Omniscient Reader's Viewpoint

Omniscient Reader's Viewpoint

01

singNsong

NEW YORK

Omniscient Reader's Viewpoint 01

singNsong

Translation by Hye Young Im and J. Torres
Cover art by BLACKBOX

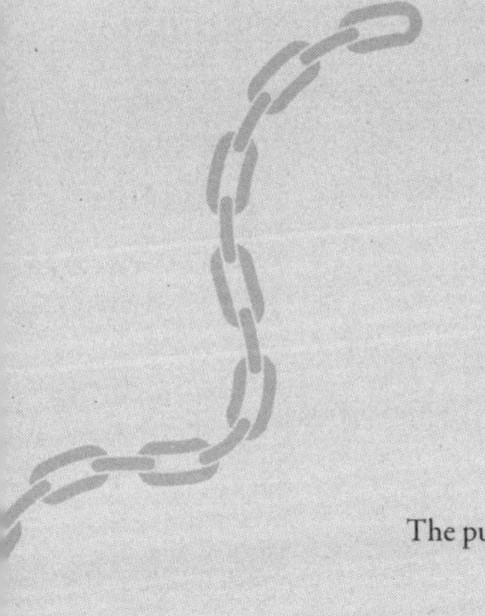

Ize Press
150 West 30th Street, 6th Floor
New York, NY 10001

Visit us at izepress.com
facebook.com/izepress
twitter.com/izepress
instagram.com/izepress

First Ize Press Edition: July 2025
Edited by Ize Press Editorial: Stephen Kim
Designed by Ize Press Design: Wendy Chan

Library of Congress Cataloging-in-Publication Data is available.

ISBNs: 979-8-4009-0352-6 (paperback)
979-8-4009-0353-3 (ebook)

3 5 7 9 10 8 6 4

TPA

Printed in South Korea

Contents

PROLOGUE

Three Ways to Survive the Apocalypse

There are three ways to survive the apocalypse. I've forgotten some of them. But one thing is for certain. If you are reading this, you will survive.

Three Ways to Survive the Apocalypse The End

My old smartphone seemed to struggle to push up the page as I swiped at the web novel app. I scrolled up and down, again and again, trying to refresh.

"Really? That's it?"

But no matter how many times I checked, the words at the bottom didn't change—*The End*.

The novel had ended.

* * *

Three Ways to Survive the Apocalypse
Author: tls123
Number of chapters: 3,149

* * *

Three Ways to Survive the Apocalypse, *TWSA* for short, was a fantasy epic spanning a whopping 3,149 chapters.

I'd been reading it since I was in ninth grade. When the bullies at school chose me to be their punching bag; when I blew my entrance exams and ended up at a third-rate college; when I drew the short stick for my military service and got stationed near the border. *Even now, as I barely hold on to my contract position after going from job to job…*

Damn it, this is depressing. Anyway…

> Author's note: Thank you for reading *TWSA*. I'll be back with the epilogue.

"Oh, there's still the epilogue. Then I guess the next chapter will be the real ending?"

It had been one hell of a journey. I'd started it over a decade ago as a child, and here I was, finishing it as a working adult.

I felt a mixture of hollowness at seeing the end of a world, and satisfaction at getting to witness that world's completion. I began to type out my comment for the last chapter, trying to find the right words.

```
Dokja Kim: Thank you so much for everything. I'm looking forward to the epilogue.
```

I truly meant it. "*TWSA* was the novel of my life." "It may not be very popular, but *TWSA* is my all-time favorite." There were many things I wanted to say, but I couldn't bring myself to write them out.

```
Average views: 1.9
Average comments: 1.08
```

That was the popularity index for *TWSA*.

It had gotten off to a decent start, with the first chapter getting twelve hundred views. But it dropped to just one hundred and twenty as it passed the Chapter 10 mark. By the time Chapter 50 came out, only twelve people were still reading it. Since Chapter 100, that number had mostly been stuck at one.

```
Number of views: 1
```

* * *

There were a few twos mixed in every now and then, but those were most likely misclicks. As I looked through the long line of ones on the chapter list, a feeling welled up in my chest.

I was grateful.

Despite only having one reader, the story had continued for over three thousand chapters, for over ten years. It wouldn't be an exaggeration to say this was a story just for me.

`Recommending an awesome novel`

I clicked on the "Recommendations" board and began typing. The author had serialized the entire novel for free. The least I could do was drop a rec. As soon as I clicked submit, people began to comment.

```
I think this guy's a troll. Checked his post history,
   and he keeps recommending the same novel.
You're the author, aren't you? You're not supposed to rec-
   ommend your own work here, you know? That's just sad.
```

I'd forgotten that I'd posted the same recommendation a few months ago. In no time, there were dozens of comments calling me a "troll" or "loser." I scrambled to delete my post but got a message saying that it couldn't be deleted because someone had already reported it.

"Oh no…"

I felt terrible that my attempt to help the author might end up making them look bad.

If people would just give it a chance, they'd be in for a real treat… Why was no one reading this gem? I wished I could donate some money to the writer, but as someone who lived paycheck to paycheck, I couldn't afford it.

It was at that moment that I got a notification: DM received.

`tls123: Thank you.`

* * *

The message had come out of nowhere. It took me a second to process what was happening.

`Dokja Kim: Aren't you the author?`

tls123.

It was the author of *TWSA*.

`tls123: I was able to finish the story thanks to your support. I even won a prize in a contest.`

I couldn't believe it.

Won a prize? *TWSA*?

`Dokja Kim: Congrats! What kind of contest was it?`
`tls123: It's an obscure one. I doubt you've heard of it.`

I thought they might have been lying to save face. But I hoped it was true. I mean, who knows? The novel had been a flop on this platform, but it could very well be a hit on another. Sure, I'd feel a bit sad about it, but a good story like this needed to get out there.

`tls123: I'd like to send you a special present as a token of my gratitude.`
`Dokja Kim: A present?`
`tls123: Yes. After all, you're the reason this story could come out into the world.`

The writer asked for my e-mail, so I gave them the one I used the most.

`tls123: By the way, the novel will be paid content soon.`

Dokja Kim: Wow, really? From when? To be honest, I should've been paying for this masterpiece from the beginning.

A new chapter of *TWSA* had been uploaded almost daily, so I would've spent about three thousand won a month. Enough for a packaged lunch from a convenience store.

tls123: It'll become paid content after today.
Dokja Kim: Does that include the epilogue that's coming out tomorrow?
tls123: I'm sorry, but yes.
Dokja Kim: Of course you should charge for it! I'll be sure to buy the chapter!

There was no further reply from the author. They seemed to have logged out. I felt a pang of disappointment. *So now that they're successful, they won't even bother replying to me, huh?* My excitement turned into petty jealousy. Why was I so happy for the novel? It wasn't like I'd written it.

"They probably sent me a gift certificate. I hope it's one that's worth fifty thousand won."

How naive I was, poring over something so trivial...

...completely clueless about what would happen to the world the following day.

EPISODE

01

The Beginning of Paid Content

Omniscient Reader's Viewpoint

1

"I'm Dokja."

That's how I introduce myself to other people. "Dokja" being an unusual name and a homonym that can mean "only child" or "reader," they often misunderstand.

"Ah, so you're an only child, huh?"

"I am, but that's not what I meant."

"Huh? Then…?"

"That's my name—Dokja Kim."

Dokja Kim. My father had named me that, hoping I'd be strong even when alone. But his wish must've only partially come true, because I ended up just alone. Here's the gist of it—

Dokja Kim. Twenty-eight years old. Single.

Hobby: reading web novels on the way home from work.

"You'll fall into your phone if you stare at it so hard."

A friendly voice cut through the noise of the subway car. I looked up to see a pair of curious eyes staring down at me. It was Sangah Yu from HR.

"Oh, good afternoon."

"Are you headed home?"

"Yes. And you, Sangah?"

"Yup. Got lucky today. My manager's on a trip."

The person next to me got off, and Sangah plopped down on the empty seat. A gentle scent wafted from her as our shoulders touched, and despite myself, I tensed up a bit.

"Do you usually take the subway?"

"Oh, about that..."

Sangah's expression darkened. I realized this was the first time I'd run into her on the subway.

Makes sense. After all, it was no secret that, from Mr. Kang in HR to Manager Han in finance, there was a whole line of men eager to give her a ride home. But I wasn't expecting what she said next.

"...someone stole my bike."

Bike?

"You ride a bike to work?"

"Yup! I've been working late these days, so I need the exercise. And...let's just say it's one less thing to worry about."

Aha, I see.

Sangah smiled. Seeing her up close, I could see why so many guys had a crush on her. Well, not that it had anything to do with me. Sangah Yu and I lived in different genres.

That seemed to be the end of the awkward conversation, and we both looked at our phones. I went back to the web novel I'd been reading earlier, and Sangah...what *was* she looking at?

"¿Puede prestarme dinero?"

"Sorry, what?"

"It's Spanish."

"...I see. What does that mean?"

"It means 'can you lend me some money?'"

Sangah answered me confidently. This woman studied on the subway. She really did live in a different genre. But what use could she have for learning Spanish anyway?

"You're studying hard."

"And what about you? What're you so focused on?"

"Oh, I'm just..."

Before I could do anything, Sangah's eyes darted to my phone screen.

"Is that a novel?"

"Yes, I'm, uh...studying Korean."

"Wow, I love novels, too. It's been a while since I read one, though. Don't have the time these days…"

That's unexpected. Sangah Yu is into this kind of stuff, too?

"You know, like Murakami Haruki, Raymond Carver, Han Kang…"

Ah, of course.

"Who's your favorite author, Dokja?"

"I doubt you've heard of them."

"Hey, I've read a lot of novels, you know? Tell me, who wrote that?"

In moments like this, I wished I had a different hobby. I glanced at the title of the web novel on my phone.

The World After the Fall
Author: singNsong

There was no way I was telling her "I'm reading *The World After the Fall* by singNsong."

"It's just a fantasy novel. Kinda like, uh…*The Lord of the Rings.*"

Sangah's eyes widened.

"Oh. *The Lord of the Rings.* I saw the movie."

"It was a good movie."

There was a brief silence. Sangah was looking at me like she expected me to continue the conversation.

It was getting awkward, so I decided to change the subject.

"Wasn't it around this time last year that we started at this company? Can't believe it's been a year already. Time flies."

"Right? We were so clueless back then, weren't we?"

"Totally. Feels like it was just yesterday, but our contracts are almost up."

It was only after seeing her expression that I realized I'd picked the wrong subject.

"Oh. Actually, I'm…"

I'd forgotten.

Sangah had been promoted to a permanent position in recognition of her role in securing a foreign contract last month.

"Oh, right. Sorry I didn't congratulate you earlier. Ha-ha. Guess I should've studied another language like you."

"D-don't worry, Dokja! There's still the performance evaluation. I'm sure you'll—"

I hated to admit it, but Sangah really was amazing. She shined like all the spotlights in the world were focused on her.

If this were a work of fiction, she'd be the heroine.

This was the logical outcome. I hadn't made an effort, and Sangah had. I'd read web novels, and she'd studied. So naturally, she'd gotten promoted, and I was to be let go.

"Um…Dokja."

"Yes."

"If you want…I can tell you what app I use to…"

Sangah's voice sounded distant. I could feel myself drifting away from the moment. I tried to bring my mind back to the present by blinking hard and staring straight ahead. There was a boy seated on the other side of the subway. Around ten years old. He was sitting next to his mom and looking down at the bug cage on his lap with gloomy eyes.

"…Dokja?"

What if I'd led a different life from this one?

Maybe if the genre of my life were different…

"Hey, Dok—"

In other words, if the genre weren't realism, but rather fantasy…could I be the hero?

I didn't know.

And I never would. But something I did know was…

"That's okay, Sangah."

"Huh?"

"It won't matter if you show me the foreign language app."

…that the genre of my life was undeniably "realism"…

"After all, Dokja lives Dokja's life."

…and that I was just a reader, not the hero.

"Dokja's life…"

Sangah had a serious look on her face. I waved my hand to reassure her

I really was fine. I didn't know her well, but it was clear she was genuinely worried about me. After all, she was in HR…so she would've had no illusions about my chances in the performance evaluation.

"What a great line!"

"Huh?"

"That means I should live Sangah's life."

This seemed to strengthen her determination about something, and she went back to studying Spanish with redoubled focus. I stared at her for a little bit before returning to the web novel.

Everything was back to normal, but for some reason, my thumb felt heavy as I scrolled through the story.

Perhaps it was the weight of my reality dragging it down—the cold, hard fact of life I'd been freshly reminded of.

It was at that moment a notification popped up on my phone.

`You've received new e-mail.`

The sender was the author of *TWSA*. I opened it right away.

```
Dear Dokja,
TWSA will be paid content starting at 7 p.m. today. This
   should help. Best of luck.
[1 Attached File]
```

Right, the author had said they'd be sending me a present. Was this it?

……I really must be a reader through and through. Getting all excited over a single e-mail…

Yeah, I guess it's not so bad to live as a reader.

I checked the time. 6:55 p.m.

That meant it would be exactly five minutes until the novel became paid content. I opened my favorites list on the novel app. As the only reader, I felt I should leave a congratulatory comment to encourage the author. However…

`No Results Found.`

* * *

I typed "apocalypse" several times into the search bar, but the result was the same.

TWSA's comment section had completely disappeared as well.

That's strange. I knew it was becoming paid content, but shouldn't there have been a notice at least?

Just then, the lights inside the subway went out, and the car was plunged into darkness.

Screeeeech!

The subway car shook violently, and the sound of grinding metal pierced my ears. Sangah clutched my arm with a small yelp of fright. She gripped so hard that the pain drowned out the ongoing chaos.

It took about ten seconds for the emergency brakes to bring the train to a full stop. Confused voices broke out all around me.

"Huh? What happened?"

"What's going on?"

Smartphones lit up one by one in the dark. Sangah spoke up, still firmly holding on to my arm.

"Wh-what was that?"

I tried my best to sound calm.

"Don't worry. I'm sure it's nothing."

"You think so?"

"Yeah, I mean, what could possibly— Well, I'm sure the operator will let us know soon."

As if on cue, the announcement came on.

`Attention, all subway passengers. Attention, all subway passengers.`

The people around us quieted down to listen. I added reassuringly, "See? It's nothing. They'll apologize about the inconvenience, and the lights will—"

* * *

E-everyone, please evacuate… I repeat, everyone—

The announcement cut off with a loud beep. And suddenly, it was chaos.

"D-Dokja? What in the world is—?"

There was a flash of bright light in front of the car, followed by what sounded like an explosion and a ripping noise.

Something was coming toward us in the dark.

It was by sheer chance that I happened to glance at the clock in that moment.

7:00 p.m.

With a loud tick, I felt as if the whole world had stopped.

And then I heard a voice.

[The free trial period for planetary system 8612 has ended.]
[The main scenario has begun.]

At that moment, my life took on a different genre.

2

"It's a goblin!" someone exclaimed when the creature appeared.

I'm not sure why I suddenly remembered that sentence from *TWSA*.

The train, dead still on the track. The sudden power outage.

These alone shouldn't have been enough to make me feel déjà vu. Emergency stops aren't common, but they do happen. So why was it that the all-too-familiar opening of the novel kept playing in my head? Surely that couldn't be. *There's no way, right?*

That was when the front door of car 3807 suddenly opened and the lights came back on. Sangah quietly mumbled beside me.

"……a goblin?"

It felt as if a siren was going off in my head. As a novel I'd read began to overlap with reality, I felt a pang of disorientation.

Two Small Horns

A bizarre creature, covered in fuzzy hair and dressed in rags, floated in midair.

It looked too creepy to be a fairy, too evil to be an angel, and too innocent to be a demon.

Therefore, it came to be called a goblin.

And I already knew what that goblin was going to say first.

* * *

&AH#@!&AH#@!...
&AH#@!&AH#@!...

At that moment, reality and fantasy converged.

"What is it saying?"

"Is this some kinda augmented reality event?"

Despite the uneasy murmurs all around me, I felt as though I'd been thrown into another world by myself. *There's no doubt about it—that's a goblin.* In the thousands of chapters of *TWSA*, it was often this very type of creature that heralded the next tale of tragedy and bloodshed. It was Sangah's voice that woke me up from my thoughts.

"That sounded like Spanish. Should I try talking to it?"

I felt a little silly as I asked, "Do you even know what that is? Are you gonna ask it to lend you money?"

"No, but..."

It was then that we heard clearly pronounced Korean.

Ah, ah. Can you hear me now? Aw man, that Korean language patch was giving me so much trouble. Can everyone hear me?

The sound of a familiar language seemed to have a calming effect on the people. The first person to speak up was a big man in a suit.

"Hey, what's all this about?"

...Pardon?

"Is it some kinda film shoot? I'm gonna be late for my audition, you know?"

I didn't recognize him, so he must've been an aspiring actor. If I were the casting director, I'd have hired him on the spot for the energy in his voice alone. Unfortunately, the creature in front of him was not a casting director.

Aha! An audition, hmm? I see. So people are busy at this time, too. Ha-ha. Guess I should've done more research. I was told that starting the paid content at 7 p.m. would get me the most people.

"Huh? What're you talking about?"

Now, now. Please calm down, everyone. Have a seat and listen to me. I have something important to tell you!

I felt a creeping sense of dread.

"What? Hell no! Get the train moving already!"

"Somebody contact the subway operator!"

"I didn't sign up for this! Do you have a permit?!"

"Mommy, what's that? A cartoon?"

At this point, there was no more room for doubt. This was the story I was familiar with, and I knew how this was going to play out. I had to stop them, but how? People wouldn't listen to that tiny and cute CG-looking creature. All I could do was stop Sangah, who was about to get up from her seat.

"Sangah, don't move. It's dangerous."

"What?"

Her eyes went wide. I'd blurted that out, but I had no way of explaining to her all that I knew about the current situation.

Or rather, there was no need to explain it to her.

Ha-ha. You people are so noisy.

After all, the creature in front of us could be *very* persuasive.

I told you to be quiet.

The goblin slowly closed its eyes, and when it opened them again, they gleamed a dangerous shade of red. There was a sound like something bursting, and the subway went silent.

"Ah, uh, uh……"

The aspiring actor who had been on his way to an audition had a large hole in his forehead. His lips twitched, as if trying to say something, then his eyes went blank, and he fell down where he stood.

This is not a film shoot.

Again, there was a sound like a melon bursting open. This time, it was the woman who had been whining about contacting the operator.

This isn't a dream, or a novel.

One by one, people's heads began to explode, spraying blood into the air. They were the ones who'd been complaining to the goblin, yelling, or making a scene. Anyone who had made any kind of noise ended up with a hole in their head. It only took a moment for the subway car to be covered in blood.

In fact, this is not reality as you knew it! You got that? Now shut up and listen to me.

More than half the people in the car were now dead. The subway train that had been full of commuters riding back home was now filled with blood and gore from the dead bodies. People couldn't even scream anymore. They stared at the goblin, dumbstruck, like prehistoric apes frozen in terror at the sight of an apex predator.

Sangah was hiccuping from shock next to me. I quietly squeezed her shoulder as I tried to calm my own breathing.

This is real.

When I'd heard the strange message, even when the goblin had appeared, a part me had still refused believe it. But as I looked around at the blood-splattered subway car, the reality of the situation finally began to set in.

You've all had quite the cozy life, haven't you?

The goblin glanced at the priority seats. The elderly who were seated there trembled and lowered their heads under its gaze. As if to scoff at them, the goblin continued its speech.

From the day you were born, you've had a free ride! Breathing, eating, and shitting without a care in the world. Breeding like flies! Ha! What a wonderful world you've lived in!

A free ride? Not a single person here had had such a thing. This was an evening rush-hour train—everyone in this car was struggling one way or another to make a living. However, no one was foolish enough to point this out to the goblin.

Well, too bad. The good times are over. There's no such thing as a free lunch, you know? If you want a happy ending, you gotta pay for it. That's just common sense, don't you agree?

No one said anything. The only sound in the subway car was heavy breathing, as people desperately tried to stave off panic. At that moment, a man cautiously raised his hand.

"I-is it money you want?"

I wondered who on earth could be that stupid. Surprisingly, it was a familiar face.

"Sangah, isn't that Manager Han from finance?"

"...You're right."

There was no mistaking it. The man who had gotten his position through connections, the last person any new employee wanted to work under—Manager Myeongoh Han from finance. But why was he on the subway?

"How much do you want? I'll pay you. H-here's my business card."

Handing his business card to a murderous entity… Manager Han's unbelievable feat of bravery seemed to bring some hope back into people's eyes.

"As you can see, money's not an issue for me. You want a million won? Two?"

It was quite a large amount for a department manager at a small company to offer so casually. I wondered if the rumor of him being the chairman's youngest son was true after all.

Hmm, you're offering me human currency?

"Th-that's right! I don't have much cash on me right now…but if you let me go, I can pay you as much as you want."

Money's nice. Plant fiber assigned value based on what humans agreed upon.

Manager Han's face lit up. He'd apparently understood the goblin's remark as an affirmation of his belief that money could solve all problems. *How pitiful.*

"Uh, this is all I have for now. So why don't you—"

But only in *your* space-time.

"What?"

A ball of fire appeared out of thin air. The bills in Manager Han's hand went up in flames. He screamed in panic.

Those scraps of paper don't mean anything in the greater dimensions. Try that again and I'll blow your head off. Got it?

"U-ugh…"

The brief spark of hope in the people's eyes turned back into fear. Their thoughts were written clearly on their faces, like a clichéd novel.

[What's gonna happen to us now?]

And I was the only one who knew exactly how this would play out.

Haah. Your debt is accruing even as we stand here yammering away. Whatever. Let's skip the explanation and have you try making some money on your own.

The goblin's horns stretched out like antennae, and its body floated up toward the ceiling.

Soon after, I heard the messages.

[Channel #BI-7623 is open.]
[Constellations have entered the channel.]

Message windows popped up above the heads of commuters who were blinking in disbelief.

[A main scenario has arrived!]

* * *

<Main Scenario #1 - Prove Your Worth>
Category: Main
Difficulty: F
Mission: Kill one or more living creatures.
Time Limit: 30 minutes
Reward: 300 coins
Penalty for Failure: Death

* * *

The goblin's body grew transparent, and it smiled as it faded through the wall into the next subway car.

Well, then. Good luck, everyone. Please, show me a fun story.

3

The goblin disappeared, and chaos erupted as people threw themselves into whatever each of them thought was the best course of action. Some struggled to escape the car, while others tried to call the police. Sangah was one of the latter.

"The police...the police aren't answering! What should we do? What—?"

"Sangah, please, calm down."

I looked straight into her panic-stricken eyes.

"You've played our company's new game, right? The one where the world ends, leaving a small group of survivors."

"Huh? What's that got to do with—?"

"Think of it this way—we are in that game right now."

Sangah looked confused.

"A game..."

"It's simple. We just have to follow the rules."

After that, I tried to calm my own breathing.

I also needed a moment to process everything that was happening.

Three Ways to Survive the Apocalypse.

Scenes from the novel were playing out right in front of my eyes.

A goblin with its horns extended like antennae.

Dead bodies strewn on the floor like pieces of garbage.

An office worker covered in blood, shaking with fear.

An old lady desperately praying in her seat.

* * *

I carefully surveyed each scene. As if I were Neo from *The Matrix*, I observed, doubted, and finally, accepted. I had no other choice. I wasn't quite sure why, but I knew beyond any doubt—

TWSA had become reality.

Let's think. What should I do to survive in this world?

"Now, now, everyone! Stay calm. Take a deep breath."

About five minutes had passed since the goblin had left when a man stepped forward.

"Feeling better? Stop what you're doing and let me have your attention, please."

I turned around and spotted a neatly trimmed crew cut. The man stood a head taller than most people and had a muscular build to match. At the sound of his voice, the people who were talking on their phones or sobbing in terror quieted down. Mr. Crew Cut waited for everyone's attention before he spoke again.

"During a national emergency, even a small bit of disorder can lead to a lot of casualties. As such, I'll be taking control of the situation."

"Huh? Who the hell are you?"

"A national emergency? Are you shitting me?!"

The instinctive objection to the word "control" seemed to bring a few people back to their senses. The young man took out a government ID from his wallet.

"I'm a first lieutenant in the army. Unit 6502."

This had a calming effect on some of the passengers.

"A soldier. He's from the army."

However, their relief was cut short.

"I've just received a message from my unit."

People gathered around to read what was on his phone screen. I happened to be close by, so I was able to get a good look.

```
Level One national emergency declared. All personnel
  must immediately report to their unit.
```

* * *

Startled gasps broke out all around the car.

A national emergency. I'd already known that would happen, but what really surprised me was something else.

Hyeonseong Lee, first lieutenant in the army.

The person standing in front of me was *the* Hyeonseong Lee.

I knew him. This was my first time seeing his face, but I remembered his name clearly because he was a major character in *TWSA*.

Steel Blade Hyeonseong Lee.

There was even a character from the novel. I had no choice but to accept that this was happening.

"Hey, army man! What the hell is going on?"

"I've been trying to get in contact with my unit, but..."

"What about the president? What is he doing? Call the president! Hurry!"

"I'm sorry, but I'm just a soldier. I don't have a direct line to the president."

"Then how can you take charge?!"

"For everyone's safety, I ask that..."

Watching Hyeonseong Lee calmly respond to these absurd questions, I realized how accurately the novel had described his character.

But wait a minute. Is this how Hyeonseong Lee's character is introduced?

The question popped up in my head, and I felt a sense of unease. As the sole reader of *TWSA*, I was positive this wasn't how it had happened in the novel.

He's supposed to appear after the first scenario is complete.

......What's going on?

I was confused. If I could just read the novel again, then I'd know for sure.

"The prime minister's making a statement! He says it's really a Level One national emergency!"

Someone shouted, prompting everyone to take out their own smartphones. Sangah turned her phone's screen toward me.

"...Dokja, look at this."

We didn't even have to search for it because "prime minister's statement" was the top trending item at every major outlet. Besides, I already knew what the video would contain.

Attention, all citizens. A number of areas, including Seoul, are under attack by unidentified terrorists.

The speech was straightforward. The government would combat these terrorists by any means necessary, and there would be no negotiation with them. Citizens, keep calm and carry on, etc., etc....

I hadn't thought much of it while reading the novel, but now that I was actually hearing this speech, I realized how ridiculous it was.

A terrorist attack... I guess that's a convenient explanation.

"By the way, why's the prime minister making this speech? Where's the president?"

"I heard he's already dead."

"What? Really?"

"It's not confirmed, but I read some comments saying that he—"

"Then it's just bullshit. You scared me!"

Of course, I knew that it wasn't just hearsay.

"Ack! What the—?!"

The sound of gunshots suddenly rang out, causing some people to drop their phones. But the gunshots had come from the phone speakers, followed by loud crackling. In the footage, where the prime minister had once stood, there were only splatters of blood. The people in the subway car gasped in horror as they realized what had just happened.

"Th-the prime minister is..."

He had been killed. By having his head blown up on live TV.

There were few more gunshots before the video went quiet. What appeared on the screen next was the goblin.

Come on, I told you already. This is no "terrorist attack." Get real!

People were at a loss for words. All they could do was open and close their mouths like fish out of water.

You still don't get it, do you? How stupid. You think this is some kinda game?

The goblin's casual tone only added to the sense of dread. I clenched my fists tight without realizing it.

Ha-ha. Very well. According to my research, the people in this country are good at video games. Then I guess I should increase the difficulty, eh?

A large timer appeared in midair with a beep. It immediately began to count down.

[Ten minutes have been deducted from the time limit.]
[The time remaining is ten minutes.]
[If the first kill does not occur within the next five minutes, every living creature in this train car will be exterminated.]

"Wh-what? This has to be a prank, right?"

"Did everyone else hear that? Hey, did you hear that message, too?"

"Army man! What do we do now? Why aren't the police here?"

"Everyone, please, calm down and listen—"

The chaos that broke out following the goblin's announcement was far too much for Hyeonseong Lee to handle. I noticed Sangah gripping my jacket tightly. And yet, I still couldn't shake the feeling that something was off.

A key character like Hyeonseong Lee was already here. So why hadn't *he* made an appearance yet? According to the story I knew, he should've showed up by now.

"M-murder! Someone got killed in the next car!"

The windows near the passageway gave a clear view of the carnage taking place in car 3907. People blanched in horror as their eyes met the gaze of the killers in the next car over.

"We can't let 'em in! Don't let anyone come in here!"

People tried to block the door. But that was unnecessary. After all, that wasn't where their enemies were.

[Entering and exiting the car is prohibited until this scenario is complete.]

With that message, people bounced off the steel door as if they had bumped into an invisible wall.

"Wh-what the heck?"

And once again, the goblin's voice rang out.

Ha-ha. Things are getting interesting all over the place, but it looks like some people are still dragging their feet. All right, then. I'll do you a special favor. Here's a preview of what will happen to you unless you take action in the next five minutes.

A large screen appeared in midair inside the subway car. It displayed a classroom. Girls in navy uniforms were trembling in fear. A high school boy next to me mumbled as he chewed on his nails.

"Those uniforms…isn't that Taepoong Girls' High School?"

Some of the girls were working together to break down the door, while others seemed to be brainstorming ideas to escape. Young students doing everything they could to get through the scenario without killing anyone. They were much wiser than the foolish adults here. That made this scene all the more tragic.

Beep, beep, beep, beep—the alarm sound grew increasingly urgent, causing the girls to scream.

[The time limit has passed.]
[Penalty will be disbursed.]

Immediately following the announcement, the head of a student sitting in the front row exploded.

Then another one. And another. The young girls' heads blew up one by one. Screaming students ran to the windows and the door.

"No...th-this can't be happening..."

Broom and mop handles broke and the girls' nails were torn off as they rammed and clawed at the classroom door. But it would not open. No one could get out. Splat. Splat. The students' heads continued to explode.

It was at that moment one girl began strangling her friend. The victim's arms went limp as she gasped her last breath. A moment later, the screen showed nothing but the one remaining girl, looking around with a feverish fire in her eyes.

[Channel #BAY23515. Taepoong Girls' High School Class 2-B Survivor: Jihye Lee.]

The girl glared directly at the screen as it faded. The goblin's voice broke the silence that fell over the train car.

How was it? Fun, right?

The goblin exclaimed these words gleefully, but people weren't looking at the screen anymore. They were nervously glancing at each other, scrambling to put some distance between themselves and everyone else in the car. Someone screamed in disbelief.

"Damn it! What the hell is this?!"

Even Sangah let go of my arm, though she didn't try to move away from me. With both my hands free, I turned on my phone.

Why hasn't he *appeared yet?*

Things were unfolding as they had in the novel, but there were key differences that were nagging at me. The only way I could sort this out was by checking *TWSA*. But how would I possibly find that novel again? Was there a bootleg copy somewhere? *I doubt it. The novel is too unpopular for anyone to even pirate it...... No, wait.*

[1 Attached File]

Seeing the e-mail notification on my phone threw me into a daze.

Surely, it's not...... No way, right?

What I saw in my in-box left me stunned. The name of the attached file the author had sent me was…

[Three Ways to Survive the Apocalypse.TXT]

I couldn't believe it. I rubbed my eyes and stared at the screen, but the file was definitely there.

The filename extension was TXT. Had the author…seriously sent me their novel as a present?

[You have acquired an exclusive attribute.]
[Your exclusive skill slot has been unlocked.]

The messages rang in my ears as I opened the file. This was nothing to be surprised about, if the world had truly turned into that of *TWSA*. The survivors in the novel received attributes and the ability to use skills.

I tried saying "attribute window" in my head. If I really had received a skill, I needed to know what it did.

[The attribute menu cannot be opened.]

What the heck? I tried again to call up the attribute window, but still nothing.

This was unexpected. What was I supposed to do? Without the menu, I couldn't see what attribute and skills I had. They say knowing is half the battle, and I was at a huge disadvantage.

I stared blankly into empty space for a while, then gave up and decided to read the file from the author first.

[Your reading speed has increased due to your exclusive attribute.]

I didn't know what my attribute was, but it allowed me to read the entire opening of *TWSA* in under a minute.

...Found it.

I stopped scrolling when I got to a scene near the beginning, in which the main character was about to perform a certain action in the subway.

> He looked over the people gathered at the rear door of car 3707. The wheel of the lighter he held tightly felt cold to the touch. There would be no mistakes in this life. He vowed to do whatever it took to reach his goals.
>
> Fear was written plain on the people's faces.
>
> He felt no remorse. This would be over in a moment.
>
> He scanned the other passengers with cold detachment. *Fwoosh.* A small flame sparked to life at his fingertip. Then it all began.

I felt a chill down my spine, and I read the passage over and over again. Now I knew why something felt off.

"...It was 3707."

I glanced around for the number of the train car I was in.

3807.

I was in the car behind the one the main character was in. My hands trembled a little.

...Hang on. Then what's supposed to happen to the people in this car?

> Through the dirty window, he watched the chaos unfolding in car 3807. Was it too late for them? *There's nothing I can do.* After all, there would only be two survivors from that car.

Only two survivors. Everyone else here would die. And I already knew who those two people were. I looked up in a daze at Sangah Yu.

This person will probably die. And so will I.

"Dokja, over there—"

I turned to see what she was pointing at. A male student who had been leaning on the wall near the entrance had moved over to the priority seats. He had a slim build, and his hair was dyed silver. I checked the name tag on his school uniform.

Namwoon Kim. As I'd thought, it was a name I knew very well.

> *There will only be two survivors in that car—Hyeonseong Lee and Namwoon Kim. That's fine. Those two are the ones I need anyway.*

Standing in front of the priority seats, Namwoon Kim scanned the elderly seated there like a butcher deciding what to slaughter first.

"Any volunteers?"

His voice was cold with undisguised intent. An old man stammered a feeble protest.

"Wh-what do you mean—?"

"You know exactly what I'm talking about. It's time to make the right decision for everyone's sake."

One by one, the other passengers were beginning to pay attention. They seemed to understand what was about to happen. Surprisingly, it was Myeongoh Han who frowned and stepped up to Namwoon.

"You brat! Are you out of your damn mind?"

Unperturbed, Namwoon stared coldly back at Myeongoh.

"Then are *you* gonna die?"

"What…?!"

"You still don't get it, do you?"

Near the ceiling, images were still playing on the holographic screen the goblin had left behind.

```
H-help!
Gyaaaagh!
Die, damn it! Die!
```

* * *

It wasn't just this train and Taepoong Girls' High. The screen was showing live footage of people dying all over the world. I saw Hyeonseong repeatedly trying to contact his army unit, his eyes locked on the grisly footage. His phone continued to ring pointlessly. Namwoon Kim scoffed.

"Wake up. The army's not coming to save us. That means we have to choose who dies."

Some of the passengers flinched at his dry words.

"Why are you hesitating? The goblin said it—we've all had free rides. By that logic, who here has had it easy the longest?"

All eyes turned to the priority seats. The elderly passengers turned pale. Namwoon had just put into cold, hard words what everyone was thinking, but hadn't dared voice aloud.

"In this kinda situation, doesn't it make sense for the ones who've lived the longest to sacrifice themselves? Or are you gonna tell the little kid over there to die?"

The child who was clinging to her mom ducked behind her back. Namwoon smirked at the girl, then turned back to Myeongoh.

"Look, I get what you're thinking. Killing each other for survival? We're not animals. I'd agree…under normal circumstances. But does this look normal to you?"

"……"

"Think carefully. The world as you knew it is over."

Myeongoh's shoulders twitched. It wasn't just him. Something was breaking inside the people. Their thin veneer of morality was beginning to crumble. And it was Namwoon Kim's words that hammered a wedge into the crack.

"A new world needs new rules."

Namwoon Kim. A disaffected youth who'd adapted to the world of *TWSA* faster than anyone.

He turned to stare directly at the elderly passengers.

"So who's gonna do it? Unless someone volunteers in five minutes, everyone will die."

The old men and women blanched at his words.

"Well, if no one comes forward, I'll have to pick one. Let's see…"

His extended finger scanned the priority seats like a sick game of Russian roulette.

No one could stop him this time. Not Myeongoh Han…not even Hyeonseong Lee.

The soldier clenched his fists, but he could only shake them in frustration.

He, too, had made a decision.

The other passengers' faces betrayed their thoughts all too clearly. I could read them like a poorly written novel.

[If no one is killed in the next five minutes, everyone dies.]

The looks in people's eyes were changing.

[If no one is killed, then I…]

Their eyes gleamed with the most primal instinct all living creatures have. Namwoon Kim's finger finally came to a halt.

"Looks like it's been decided."

He seized the trembling woman by the collar and lifted her to her feet. He glared at the struggling elder in his clutches, then back at the other passengers.

"What're you waiting for? Are you just gonna stand there and die?"

Some looked away, while others met his gaze. The first to make a move was an office worker wearing a backpack.

"…He's right. Everyone will die if we don't do anything."

The office worker approached the old woman.

The others began to mumble as if they were possessed.

"Yes, someone has to… There's no other choice. This is the only way we'll survive."

"Gah, screw it!"

Two, then three.

The passengers who had been watching furtively moved toward the priority seating. The man who had been pacing around indecisively. The university student who was recording everything on her phone. The mother who seemed to have forgotten about her child. Even Myeongoh Han eventually joined in. They all knew—if this old lady was not killed, they'd be the ones to die. One by one, they began to lynch the defenseless woman, hesitantly at first.

"L-let's be honest, you don't have much left in you anyway! Let the young people live!"

"Just die! Die already!"

I remembered something I'd once read in a novel.

> Executioners pull the lever at the same time, so as to conceal who really ended someone's life.

I watched the scene before me as if I was reading that passage again.

Like I was spectating a commotion happening in another world.

This couldn't have been avoided. As written in the original story, that unnamed old lady was not meant to survive.

It was at this moment that Sangah bolted up from her seat. I grabbed her by reflex.

"I told you not to move."

"Dokja."

I could feel Sangah's arms trembling as I gripped them. She clenched her fists, as if to steel herself, but she couldn't stop shaking. I tried to talk her down.

"If you go there now, you'll become their target."

"I know. I know that, but…"

Her eyes were shaking with fear, but there was a spark of resolve in them.

"I can't just sit here and do nothing."

It hit me once again. *Regardless of the genre, some people are destined to shine.*

"Sangah, stay here."

However, she's not the one who can change this story. After all, she is not the heroine of this world.

"But—"

"Listen to me just this once. I won't tell you what to do again."

After forcing Sangah to sit back down, I turned around and took a deep breath. I straightened my back and breathed out slowly. I began to stretch my wrists and ankles.

To be honest, I felt it was a bit too early for me to step in. This hadn't been my original plan.

"...Dokja?"

I didn't answer her, and instead looked at the other passengers. It felt like time was slowing down as I watched Namwoon's raised fist descend. People surrounded the helpless woman like executioners carrying out the sentence together.

I wasn't standing back because I was scared of Namwoon Kim or the others, nor was it because I condoned their inhumane actions. I was simply waiting for the right moment to make my move. *And the timing is...*

Boom—!

...now.

"Ack! What was that?!"

The sound of the explosion rang in my ears, and the train shook violently from the impact. Screams everywhere. Smoke from the car in front of us was seeping into ours.

It's begun. He's made his move.

I dashed forward with all my strength, past the people crouched in terror, toward the old woman.

"What the—?! Argh!"

Namwoon Kim crashed to the ground with a scream as I rammed him head-on. It might have seemed like I'd shoved him aside to save the old lady, but that wasn't what I was after.

Where is it?

I quickly looked around. Kill or be killed—that was the law of the new world. And in the midst of this hellscape, a child was crying. It was the boy with the bug cage I had seen earlier.

"Sorry, but I'll be taking that."

I reached for the bug cage he was clutching in his arms, and the boy stepped back warily. I shook my head.

"Please."

He eventually acquiesced. I put my hand in the cage, wincing in disgust at the feel of a grasshopper's chitinous exoskeleton. I took one out and gave it to the boy. Then I turned around toward the others.

"Everyone, stop! You won't survive even if you kill her."

In the momentary silence that followed the explosion, my voice rang clearly through the whole subway car. One by one, people turned my way.

"Let's say you kill the old lady. And then what?"

It pleased me to see them flinch in surprise. I had their full attention now.

"Sure, it'll count as the 'first kill' and buy you some time. But what then?"

"Uh…"

"If the goblin was telling the truth, then each of us has to kill someone. So who will you murder? The person next to you?"

Reminded of the brutal reality by my words, the passengers shuffled away from each other, eyes darting around nervously.

Their faces were filled with fear. The truth was, they'd known all along—the old lady was just the beginning. Namwoon Kim spoke up, as if to retake control of the situation.

"What's there to worry about? Just kill that guy next! Buncha cowards. Stop fretting about the order! Half will live, and the other half will die. Simple as that!"

I'd known he'd say something like that. I waved my hand to cut him off.

"That kind of coin flip isn't necessary. There's a way for you to survive without becoming a murderer."

"What?"

"H-how?"

The crowd became agitated. Namwoon's face contorted into a scowl.

"Did you forget? The condition for clearing this scenario isn't killing a person."

Kill one or more living creatures.

There had been no mention of "human being" in the scenario description. Kill one or more living creatures. In other words, it didn't matter what you killed, as long as it lived. Someone quickly connected the dots and pointed at the bug cage I was holding.

"A bug! Look at those bugs!"

Grasshoppers and crickets were hopping around inside the cage. People's eyes narrowed. I nodded.

"That's right. Insects."

I reached inside the cage and took out a grasshopper. It was the one I'd noted earlier, with a swollen abdomen.

"G-give me that! Hurry!"

"Just one! One bug is all I want!"

I slowly stepped back, keeping my eyes on the crowd surging toward me with outstretched arms. The murderous rage that had been directed at the old woman was now turned upon me.

I felt my lips curl up into a smile.

Why? My very life is in danger, yet why does my heart beat with excitement?

"Do you want it?"

I shook the cage like a circus trainer trying to provoke a pack of savage beasts. As a few of them lost their patience and lunged at me, I crushed the grasshopper in my hand.

[You have completed the "First Kill" achievement.]
[You have received 100 coins as a bonus reward.]

The sensation of a life being squashed out filled my clenched fist.

"Then you can have it!"

At the same time, I flung the bug cage away with my other hand. I made sure to hurl it in the opposite direction of where Namwoon and the crowd were standing.

"That crazy son of a…!"

With the door of the cage flung wide open, the bugs leaped toward freedom.

4

People went into a panic as the insects hopped all around the car.

"H-hey! Why would you do such a—?"

Some people froze in shock; others quickly regained their senses and shoved past me.

"Bastard! I'll get you for this."

"...You'd better hurry and catch one. Only three minutes left."

As if on cue, the people began to ransack every corner of the subway car like crazed beasts.

"Yes! I got—! Gaah!"

The triumph of those lucky enough to catch an insect, and the murderous desperation of the less fortunate who were trying to seize the precious critters by force... Utter mayhem broke out.

"Hey, what did you do that for? You coulda just handed 'em out."

I looked to my side to see Namwoon rising to his feet.

"There are twelve people left in this car."

"......Huh?"

"And there were only three insects left in the cage."

Namwoon looked confused for a beat, then burst out laughing.

"Twelve to three? Ha-ha-ha-ha! I see. There weren't enough to go around, so you threw the whole cage. Is that it?"

"That's right."

"Don't make me laugh."

"......?"

"No one in their right mind would think of doing that."

Namwoon Kim's smile widened.

"Be honest. You just wanted to watch people fight for 'em, didn't you?"

I thought about the Namwoon Kim I knew from *TWSA*. Just then, I heard a message.

[Exclusive skill "Character Profile" has been activated.]

A window appeared before my eyes. I didn't know exactly what my attribute was, but I was starting to get an idea.

<Character Profile>
Name: Namwoon Kim
Age: 19
Sponsoring Constellation: None (Two constellations are currently interested in this character.)
Exclusive Attribute: Edgelord (Common)
Exclusive Skills: [Abnormal Adaptability Lv.3], [Knife Fighting Lv.1], [Dark Awakening Lv.1]
Total Stats: [Stamina Lv.3], [Strength Lv.4], [Agility Lv.6], [Magic Power Lv.4]
Summary: An edgy teenager who fully embraced his inner darkness following an extraordinary event. Getting involved with him is not recommended.

* * *

There were a number of teenagers with delusions of grandeur in *TWSA*. But when their edgy daydreams became actual reality, most of them weren't able to handle it and killed themselves. However, Namwoon Kim was different.

Delusional Demon Namwoon Kim.

There was a good reason he would come to be known as the "Delusional

Demon." This boy's dark fantasies went far beyond that of the average teen edgelord. He'd been waiting for the apocalypse for a long time, so when it became reality, he was able to adapt without missing a beat.

"Team up with me. What do you say?"

And here he was, making me an offer.

[Character *Namwoon Kim* expresses interest in you.]
[Your understanding of character *Namwoon Kim* has increased.]

Teaming up with Namwoon would guarantee my survival for now. Perhaps if I hadn't read *TWSA*, I'd have made a different choice.

"Sorry, but I prefer to go solo."

"For real? That's too bad."

Namwoon Kim smacked his lips and stepped toward me.

"Then get outta my way. I've got some unfinished business with granny over there."

I turned around to see what his gaze was fixed upon. The old woman lay bleeding on the ground, breathing weakly.

"Aren't you going to catch a bug?"

"You mean those grasshoppers? Why would I bother with those…"

Namwoon replied with a nasty grin.

"…when there's a bug right here that I've already caught?"

His murderous intent prickled my skin. A fictional character made up of words and sentences, yet here he was—living, breathing, and every bit as crazy as he'd been described in the novel. Despite myself, I was amazed.

Namwoon Kim really is just as I imagined him.

[Character *Namwoon Kim*'s opinion of you slightly decreases.]

"What're you gawking at? I said get outta my way."

"I'm afraid I can't do that."

"Huh?"

"I'm saying, I'm not letting you get past me."

"Ha-ha. You seriously gonna play the hero now? You have a split personality or something?"

I didn't answer him. Namwoon's face slowly darkened. The friendly interest in his eyes turned into icy disdain.

"Hang on. Is this why you threw the bug cage? This was your goal all along?"

"......"

"Just to save that granny? Ha-ha-ha! Crazy bastard! Actually insane! You're kidding, right?"

I didn't say anything. Looking at Namwoon in the flesh, I remembered...

"So you're one of those, huh? Man, I hate people like you."

...how much his character annoyed me the whole time I was reading *TWSA*.

[Character *Namwoon Kim* despises you.]

"I said, move!"

I waited for the right timing, then ducked. Namwoon had thrown a punch before finishing his sentence.

"Oh? Not bad."

Even though I'd known full well it was coming and had successfully dodged his fist, I felt a wave of heat passing above my head. It was no ordinary punch.

[Dark Awakening Lv.1]

A black aura emanated from Namwoon's body. A skill exclusive to teen edgelords.

It was rare for a character to use a skill before the first scenario was over, but Namwoon was already doing it. This was why the main character had recruited him, despite all his flaws.

Wham!

My shoulder spasmed violently where I'd taken a hit. There was no chance of me winning like this.

...*Should I use* that *now?*

I was counting down to the right moment in my head when I heard a message.

> [Your understanding of character *Namwoon Kim* has increased.]
> [You have met the conditions for using the exclusive skill "Omniscient Reader's Viewpoint" Lv.1!]

Namwoon's fist slammed down with a loud thud.

"Ha-ha, what is this? I'm strong as hell!"

The impact left a dent in the hard subway floor. Namwoon Kim was beginning to realize just how powerful he'd become. Each of his punches carried enough force to break my bones, but they kept landing on the floor instead. He shouted in frustration.

"Gaaah! Why can't I hit him?"

Of course he couldn't land a hit. It was thanks to my second skill.

> [Exclusive skill "Omniscient Reader's Viewpoint" Lv.1 has been activated.]

As soon as it had activated, I could clearly see what Namwoon was targeting, as if I was reading his mind. For example...

[Right hook]

I quickly arched my body backward beyond his reach…

[Right eye]

…then ducked forward to dodge the follow-up attack.

"Argh! Let me hit you, damn it!"

[Left thigh]

I could easily keep this up. All I had to do was stall until time ran out. I pointed at the timer as I dodged his fist.

"Two minutes left, kid."

Feeling the pressure, Namwoon glanced back and forth between me and the old woman.

"Aw, shit……!"

His eyes settled on the latter. He had made his choice. I was forced to grab her and roll away. *If she dies now, Namwoon Kim will clear the scenario. No matter what it takes, I can't let this lunatic move on to the next scenario.*

"Ha-ha, I knew you'd do that."

I had a bad feeling. Namwoon was taking something out from his backpack. The bright fluorescent light of the subway car glinted off the blade in his hand. A Swiss Army knife. I'd forgotten he was a huge military nerd.

Swish!

This was a combination of the technical skill "Knife Fighting" and the buff skill "Dark Awakening." And it was clear where the blade was aimed.

[Heart]

Even though I knew it was coming, I wouldn't be able to avoid this attack. I quickly made a decision. If I couldn't avoid it, I'd have to take it where it would do the least damage.

The blade barely missed my heart and cut into my shoulder instead.

That hurts. That really *hurts.*

It felt like my skin was on fire. My vision went blurry, and I felt like death was just a small step away.

"Ha-ha, die now!"

One minute and thirty seconds remained in the scenario. I glanced at the old lady. I felt bad for her, but now I really had no choice but to use *that*.

"Namwoon Kim, Chungil High School, eleventh grade. Let me ask you one thing."

"……Huh?"

"Does an insect's egg count as a living thing?"

I took the dead grasshopper I had killed earlier out of my pocket. I felt a bulging mass on its abdomen—a full egg sac.

Crunch, and viscous fluid spurted out.

An unpleasant wetness spread all over my hand as the messages began.

[You killed a living creature.]
[You have received 100 coins as a bonus reward.]
[You killed a living creature.]

……

[You killed a living creature.]
[You have received 100 coins as a bonus reward.]

Countless messages rang in my ears.

Namwoon Kim scowled.

"An insect's egg? What the hell are you talking about? Trying to buy time?"

"In a way."

"How the hell would I know? I always slept through biology class."

Namwoon looked at my bloodied shoulder and grinned.

"But there's one thing I do know. Wanna hear it?"

"What?"

"You're gonna die now!"

Before he'd even finished speaking, he lunged at me with the knife. Another attack I wouldn't be able to dodge.

[You have obtained a large number of coins! Would you like a tutorial on coin usage?]

I skipped the explanation. No need to hear it, since I already knew.

"No, you're the one who'll die."

I retorted, then muttered a series of instructions.

[You have invested 2,700 coins on stamina.]
[Stamina Lv.1 → Stamina Lv.10]
[Your stamina stat has increased greatly.]
[Physical durability has increased greatly.]

Namwoon Kim's Swiss Army knife pierced my heart.

Or rather, it looked like it should have.

However, his attack only left a small scratch on my skin, as if he'd tried to stab a rock. His eyes widened with shock.

"How?!"

"I'll give you the answer to my question. An insect's egg is a living thing."

"Wh-what?"

"And during spawning season, a single grasshopper can lay more than a hundred eggs."

An egg. A living thing. One hundred of them.

Sadly, there wasn't enough time for Namwoon's dim brain to process that information.

"What the hell are you talking about?"

"I didn't think you'd understand. One minute left now."

Finally, fear spread across his face.

"Gaaah! I'll kill you! Die!"

This time, his knife came directly for my neck. I didn't block his attacks on purpose.

Kriiik!

Perhaps it was because he'd stabbed the skin on my neck this time rather than my chest, but it left a deeper scratch than before. But it still didn't hurt.

"Namwoon Kim."

Behind his flailing arms, I could see the other passengers still scrambling to catch the bugs. When it came to their own survival, they wouldn't hesitate to hurt others.

"You were right. You and I are not so different."

Perhaps I could've saved those people.

"Shit! Die! Why won't you die?!"

Fifty-five seconds. Fifty seconds. Forty-five seconds.

The knife could only scratch me. Though his attacks drew some blood, his blade failed to cut into my flesh. It was thirty seconds before the time limit when Namwoon opened his mouth and spoke again. He dropped his knife and knelt before me.

"H-help me."

Twenty-five seconds.

"Please help me, mister! I'm begging you! Please!"

"Why should I?"

Twenty seconds.

"Because human life is precious! You're supposed to help others in need!"

"Maybe that's how it was in the old world. But you said it yourself—a new world needs new rules."

Ten seconds.

"N-no! I don't wanna die! Damn it! Aaaah!"

Five seconds.

Namwoon screamed and lunged at me, his knife aimed at my eye.

The moment his blade was about to pierce my retina—

[The time limit has expired.]

Splat! Namwoon Kim's head exploded.

[Proceeding to checkout.]

One after another, people's heads blew up throughout the subway car.

One, two, three, four...

Their heads exploded like fireworks announcing the beginning of the new world.

I watched this gruesome spectacle with a mixture of exhilaration, guilt, and a strange sense of dissociation.

How?

How was it that I could be so calm watching this macabre scene?

As if I was reading a novel.

[You have massacred 124 living creatures.]
[Your kills: 1 grasshopper and 123 grasshopper eggs.]
[Because you only killed helpless creatures that offered no resistance, your earnings are halved.]
[You have obtained 6,200 coins.]
[The coins you used to upgrade your stats are automatically deducted.]
[You have obtained a total of 3,500 coins.]
[Due to your gratuitous massacre, you have unlocked the "Mass Murderer" achievement.]

I could see my face reflected in the darkened subway window.

In all the countless times I'd looked into the mirror, I'd never seen such an expression on my own face.

I wiped at the blood on my cheek, but it wouldn't come off. Then I realized the blood was on the window.

With a lurch, the train began moving again. It clunked at regular intervals as it ran along the tracks. Soon, sunlight shined through and drove out the darkness. It was the aboveground section of Line 3, between Apgujeong and Oksu. The scenery of Seoul and the Han River could be seen out the windows.

"Ahh."

Someone moaned, overcome with emotion. A sound filled with the relief of having survived. However, it wasn't long before the triumph in their voice turned into something else.

"Ah, ah…"

The scene outside the windows wasn't the Seoul we knew.

Smoke and dust everywhere. The city was in ruins.

The bridges spanning the Han River had collapsed.

On either side of the water stained red with the blood of dead soldiers, the riverbanks were littered with the debris of fallen buildings, and gigantic monsters were crushing K1 tanks underfoot like they were toys.

[Main Scenario #1 - Prove Your Worth has ended.]
[You have obtained 300 coins as the standard reward for clearing the scenario.]
[100 coins were deducted for channel usage fee.]
[Bonus rewards are being calculated.]

One world has died, and another has been born.
And I'm the only one who knows how this world ends.

EPISODE
02

Main Character

Omniscient Reader's Viewpoint

1

The train came to a stop about halfway across Dongho Bridge.

"Goodness..."

The few surviving passengers got up and looked outside. Seoul in ruins and covered in fallen buildings. Gigantic serpentlike monsters devouring the wreckage of a crashed fighter jet.

"Wh-what are those things...?"

I recognized them right away.

Angler dragons.

They were commonly known as sea serpents. In the future, these creatures would be classified as level-7 monsters. One of the angler dragons turned toward us.

"A-ack! It's coming!"

The survivors yelled in terror. But I calmly watched the fearsome creature swim toward us. I knew it wasn't a threat to us.

Kraaaah!

The sea serpent roared and spun around Dongho Bridge. Then it disappeared underwater, leaving bubbles in its wake.

In the world of TWSA, *the scenarios take priority above all else. That means we'll be protected as long as we're playing our parts. Those monsters won't attack us. Not now, at least.*

[Due to an unexpected review of the scenario, the calculation of your rewards is being delayed. Thank you for your patience.]

The rewards should've been distributed by now, but there was nothing but this error message floating in midair.

It was probably because of me.

I looked at Namwoon Kim's headless body. According to *TWSA*, he was supposed to kill most of the people in this car and move on to the next scenario.

But I'd stopped that from happening.

If I was right, it was about time for them to appear—the ones who were angered by Namwoon's death.

[Two constellations express displeasure with you over the death of character *Namwoon Kim*.]

Constellations.

They were the most mysterious beings in the world of *TWSA*, the masterminds behind all its tragedies. Seeing the messages of their reactions reminded me that the main game was about to start.

What a joke. Just yesterday, I'd been the one reading about them, but now our positions had been flipped.

[A small number of constellations are impressed by your scenario.]
[They have donated 500 coins.]

Just as some despised me, others liked what they were seeing.

I wasn't happy with either of those prospects, but there was nothing I could do about it at the moment.

After all, I was their clown now, forced to dance for their entertainment.

As I picked up Namwoon's Swiss Army knife from the ground, I thought to myself...

Watch me all you want. Eventually, you'll be paying for it with your lives.

"...Dokja? Are you okay?"

I looked up to see Sangah's face. Shoulders drooping listlessly. Bloodstains on her white blouse. Torn stockings. The Sangah Yu I'd once known was no more. I took her hand and stood up.

"I'm sorry. I couldn't save the old lady."

I looked down at the old woman's headless body. I didn't even know her name. From here on, countless people would die like this.

Sangah looked torn as she gazed at me.

"Dokja, how are you able to—"

"Hmm?"

"N-never mind. Anyway...thank you for earlier."

"For what?"

"You know. Earlier, you..."

Then I remembered.

Sangah had been standing near where I'd thrown the bug cage. I knew what she was thinking.

"It was just a coincidence. Don't expect it to happen again."

"Oh......"

She nodded without saying a word. I couldn't tell what was going through her head, but she was a smart woman. I was sure she understood.

Some had lived while others had died, because of my choice.

I didn't deserve any thanks from those who'd survived.

Whoa, this is crazy.

The goblin appeared in midair with a crackling noise.

What on earth happened here? I was checking up on another car for just a sec, and......

The goblin's face was a mixture of joy and shock. There were starlike points of light floating above its fuzzy head.

I counted how many there were. One, two, three…twenty, twenty-one. Twenty-one in total, huh? No wonder that bastard looked so pleased.

I can't believe twenty-one of you are tuning in… Is this my lucky break? Ooh, a donation, even! Thank you, constellations. Ha-ha, everyone! Looks like you earned your keep.

The number of stars represented the number of constellations who were tuned in to the channel. Twenty-one wasn't a lot, but it must've been a record for this rookie goblin.

Well, well, well. That's quite a lot of survivors. That guy in the next car was one crazy bastard, too…… Got some great stories today.

The goblin gloated, then fiddled with some invisible controls. Soon, the list of survivors came up.

[Survivors of Train 3442 to Bulgwang - Car 3807: Dokja Kim, Hyeonseong Lee, Sangah Yu, Gilyeong Lee, Myeongoh Han. Total: 5 survivors.]

Five survivors. More than I'd expected.

I scanned their faces one by one. I'd known Hyeonseong would make it because he was strong and athletic. I'd expected Sangah to survive as well.

And Gilyeong Lee.

I surmised that was the name of the boy standing next to me. There was a crushed grasshopper in his hand, the one I'd given to him.

The boy stared silently at the headless corpse of his mother. She had abandoned him to join in the killing of the old woman. And he had watched the whole thing.

I hesitated for a bit, then put my hand on his shoulder. This wasn't some cheap sympathy. If I had to describe what I was doing, I'd call it… hypocrisy.

"Hey, kid."

The boy slowly looked up, his eyes filled with fear. The shock of his first brush with death hadn't worn off yet.

"Do you wanna live?"

His pupils shook nervously. His body trembled as if he was trying to resist an irresistible power. Then, almost imperceptibly, he nodded.

"Then come with me."

Gilyeong scurried over and clung to my leg. Sangah watched this moving scene with a tender expression. *Seems like I've caused another misunderstanding.* Well, I had meant to make a show of it, though not for Sangah.

[A small number of constellations are touched by your kindness.]
[They have donated 200 coins.]

Some might have called it a dirty trick, but what can I say? I had to do everything I could to survive. Considering the crucial event that was coming up, now was the time to get the constellations' attention.

Someone shouted.

"Th-then you're letting us go? We did as you told us to, didn't we?"

It was Myeongoh, who was standing a few feet away from me, his shirt in tatters.

Manager Myeongoh Han. He was one lucky guy, I'll give him that. But I was puzzled. What was a rich man like him doing on a subway train anyway?

Just a short while ago, he'd been bragging to the whole company about his new Mercedes.

Hmm, let you go? Have you looked outside? Sure you wanna go out there?

The goblin chuckled.

Anyway, I'm quite impressed. To be honest, I didn't expect much from this car, but you made it past the first scenario. You've shown me that even insects deserve a chance.

Its words reminded me of the position we were in. We were nothing but grasshoppers in the goblin's eyes.

Now, now. You should be rewarded for pushing through, right? For clearing the first scenario, you've earned the privilege of being sponsored by constellations. Wow! Isn't that exciting? ...Hmm, you don't seem very excited. This is a huge deal, you know?

Of course they weren't excited. "Constellations," "sponsor"… I was the only one here who knew what those words meant. And I knew exactly what the goblin was leading up to. Sponsor Selection. One of the key events in *TWSA* was about to begin.

Hmm, everyone looks confused. Let me explain. You're very weak right now. Pathetic, really. If you go into the next scenario in your current state, a ground rat would easily kill you, never mind a kruk. But thankfully, there are great and magnanimous beings in this universe who pity you and are willing to sponsor you. Now do you get it?

Hopelessly lost, Hyeonseong blurted out, "What does any of that mean? Who's sponsoring wh—?"

Seriously? This is not rocket science, damn it. Fine. I'm not gonna float here explaining all day. Why don't you just see for yourselves? Well, I guess some of you won't even get the chance, but whatever. Ha-ha-ha.

I tensed up with anxiety. *This is where is all starts. I need to make the right choice here if I'm to survive.*

"Um, Dokja? Something just popped up. Two weird choices…"

"I don't know. You're on your own."

Of course, that was a lie to avoid suspicion.

Still, two choices? I guess Sangah had gotten lucky, too.

"Don't stress over it too much. Think of it as an aptitude test."

"An aptitude test…"

"No one really knows what's going on. So let's keep an open mind and roll with it."

"Oh…okay."

That seemed to convince Sangah, and she stared intently at the empty space in front of her. Her brow furrowed, as if she were trying to decipher a cryptic horoscope.

Everyone else had gone quiet, too. They were likely reading through their own choices.

I turned my eyes back to my own options as well.

* * *

<Sponsor Selection>
Choose your sponsor.
The chosen sponsor will be your trusty supporter.

1. Abyssal Black Flame Dragon
2. Demonic Judge of Fire
3. Secretive Plotter
4. Prisoner of the Golden Headband

* * *

Four choices that sounded like riddles.

This meant that four constellations wanted to make me their incarnation.

Considering the main character of *TWSA* got five offers, four wasn't bad at all. And what really mattered wasn't the number of choices, but the cryptic words next to those numbers.

Constellations never revealed their true names.

The trick was to consider key words such as "Abyssal" and "Demonic" to deduce their true identities. Of course, this was a piece of cake for someone like me, who'd read the novel.

First, "Abyssal Black Flame Dragon."

* * *

According to my memory, this was a powerful being at the head of Black Cloud, a syndicate of constellations.

I couldn't remember its true name—only that it was extremely long.

A contract with this constellation grants a powerful boost to one's combat abilities, making it a great option early on when you're sorely lacking in stamina and strength.

Of course, this early advantage doesn't come without a price.

Using this constellation's power gradually pollutes the mind, eventually turning you into a psychopathic murderer. It had an affinity for delusional edgelords… I thought it ended up being Namwoon Kim's sponsor in the novel.

Too shady. I'll pass.

Second, "Demonic Judge of Fire."

I was kinda moved that this one was on my list.

Their epithet had some sinister words in it. But the term "Demonic" was a trick. If you think about it, "Demonic" means that it's not actually a demon. And then there are the key words "Fire" and "Judge." In summary, it's a being that passes judgment with fire.

Ironically, this constellation was an angel. If I remembered correctly, it was the Archangel Uriel…

Not a bad choice at all, but I'll hold off for now. Constellations of the absolute good alignment are powerful, but also come with a slew of ridiculous restrictions.

Third, "Secretive Plotter."

Even I had never seen this one before. They might've been mentioned in passing… But I wasn't sure. Maybe I'd find something once I gave *TWSA* another thorough read.

What was clear was that they probably weren't that strong. Putting aside the weak-sounding descriptors, the name didn't seem to have any ties to a major legend or myth, as far as I could tell.

"Secretive Plotter"? It didn't have the gravitas of an epithet describing a powerful constellation. *Pass.*

And lastly, "Prisoner of the Golden Headband."

My heart skipped a beat as soon as I saw the fourth choice. I couldn't believe I'd gotten an offer from this one so early on. I thought I might've read it wrong, but no.

There was no mistake: It was "Prisoner of the Golden Headband."

"Prisoner" didn't sound that great at first glance, but the proper noun was the key here.

The "Golden Headband"—the smallest prison in the world.

Anyone who'd read *Journey to the West* would have gotten the hint easily. In all the folk traditions and literature in the world, there is only one being imprisoned by a golden headband.

The master of Mount Huaguo, who suffers from the pain of a fetter squeezing into his head. The Handsome Monkey King with fiery eyes and a golden gaze.

The Great Sage, Heaven's Equal. Sun Wukong.

There was a character in the novel sponsored by this being.

The mighty constellation who swept away hundreds of incarnations with a single swing of his golden staff and slew thousands of monsters with a bolt of lightning. I still got goose bumps thinking about the author's vivid description of his prowess.

I wasn't sure why this powerful constellation had taken an interest in me, but I knew that if I had "the Great Sage, Heaven's Equal" as my sponsor, I could easily survive this new world. However…

I quietly stared at the door which connected our car to the one in front of ours. I could picture *him* standing past that door, reading through a message similar to the one that was in front of me.

If I chose "the Great Sage, Heaven's Equal," would I be able to beat him?

[Sponsor Selection will end in one minute.]

Time was ticking.
I took a small breath as I looked over my choices one last time.
It didn't take me long to make a decision.

2

[Sponsor Selection has ended.]

I took a deep breath and read the messages that popped up.

[A number of constellations are shocked by your choice.]

Ah, here we go.

[Constellation *Abyssal Black Flame Dragon* is furious about your decision.]
[Constellations affiliated with Black Cloud share *Abyssal Black Flame Dragon*'s anger. You will not receive donations from them for a time.]

No surprises there. I'd known they'd react this way.
Turning his whole posse against me just because I'd rejected his offer……

That was Namwoon Kim's original sponsor, all right. Like constellation, like incarnation.

[Constellation *Demonic Judge of Fire* is disappointed in you.]
[She will closely monitor your sense of justice from now on.]

Archangel Uriel was simply disappointed. It was rare for constellations of the absolute good alignment to outright hate someone unless they'd committed some grave sin.

[Constellation *Secretive Plotter* is intrigued by your choice.]
[They have donated 200 coins.]

I wasn't expecting Secretive Plotter's reaction at all. Judging by their epithet, perhaps they thought highly of my shrewdness.

[Constellation *Prisoner of the Golden Headband* is amused by your choice.]

And the Great Sage, Heaven's Equal...

I didn't know how to feel about this one. Had I made the right choice? I wasn't sure. I might have squandered an incredible opportunity.

[You have not chosen a sponsoring constellation.]

Having a sponsor could be a great boon, but it also limited your potential. After all, a contract with a constellation wasn't a fair agreement.

I'm going to survive. But I won't do so at the cost of becoming their plaything.

And if I was right, there were other ways to gain power without choosing a sponsoring constellation. Perhaps even stronger than those with top-tier sponsors.

Ha-ha, oh boy... Someone has made an interesting choice, I see. Well, all right. There will be another chance.

The goblin's eyes narrowed, then lingered on me for a moment.

Well, then. You've made your selections, so why don't you take a quick break while I prepare the next scenario? See you in ten minutes!

Once Sponsor Selection was over, the goblin disappeared. Although it had said to take a break, these ten minutes would be crucial. I had to use that time to take stock of the situation and prepare for the next scenario.

"Character Profile" and "Omniscient Reader's Viewpoint."

I still wasn't sure exactly how to use them, but I had a decent grasp on what they did. That was enough for now.

"Please, gather around."

The survivors, who had been eyeing each other nervously, came together at my words. Hyeonseong Lee was the first to extend his hand and introduce himself.

"Hello, I'm Hyeonseong Lee."

"I'm Dokja Kim."

"I wish…it had been under different circumstances, but it's nice to meet you. As I said, I'm a soldier…or rather, I was one."

"Still can't contact your unit?"

"…No."

I could feel his strength through our firm handshake. As expected of a top-tier vanguard in *TWSA*. I had to get Hyeonseong Lee on my team, no matter what. *He may not look like much right now, but he's a crucial character in the later parts of* TWSA.

"Oh, and Dokja…"

"Yes?"

"Thank you for earlier. We'd all be dead if it weren't for your actions."

"No, that was—"

"Even if we'd survived, we would've lost our humanity. Thank you again. And…I'm ashamed."

Hyeonseong made a bow in gratitude. I felt a bit torn. After all, this man would've survived even if I hadn't done anything. Just then, someone grabbed my shoulder.

"Ha-ha, that's our temp for you. Good job. You know who I am, right?"

I could tell who it was without even looking. I took his hand off my shoulder as I spoke.

"Yes, Myeongoh Han."

"Excuse me? That's Manager Han to you."

Even in this situation, this guy's trying to assert his seniority. That's Myeongoh Han, all right.

"We're not at the office, in case you haven't noticed."

"Ha! You tryna get fired? Did nobody teach you manners?"

Watching his tantrum hammered home the fact that the world I'd once known had truly ended. This man had been a predator at the top of the food chain before this scenario began. And I had been nothing but prey at the mercy of his kind. That was how it had been just a short while ago.

"And don't get me started about that nonsense earlier. You should've told me about the bugs first. How could you just throw them?"

"…"

"Get your priorities straight, Dokja. You'd do well to get in my good graces. Your contract is up soon, isn't it? Don't you know what a crucial time—"

It's funny. The structure of the world I'd lived in was such a fragile thing.

"Myeongoh."

"Eh?"

"Shut up already."

"Wh-what?"

"Do you still not get it? Maybe I should've let that kid beat some sense into you. Mino Soft? Look outside. You think that company still exists?"

Myeongoh turned pale, mouth agape like a fish out of water. I turned toward the others. I needed to make things perfectly clear to everyone else, too.

"And not just Myeongoh. You all need to wake up. As the goblin said, this is not a joke."

"……"

"I'm sure you've realized by now. Attribute menu, exclusive skills, an interface like a video game. Is there anyone who hasn't figured it out yet?"

As I expected, no one raised their hand. Internet and technology were a major part of daily life in Korea, so most people had played an RPG at least once. Even those who hadn't must've read fantasy novels or webcomics.

Hyeonseong sighed.

"It's just like the novels I read during night shifts. I still can't believe it. Am I dreaming?"

"No, this is real."

At my dry response, something seemed to shift in his eyes.

[Character *Hyeonseong Lee* feels a faint trust toward you.]
[Your understanding of character *Hyeonseong Lee* has increased.]

He nodded.

"You don't mince words. I like that. Then what should we do next? Do you have something in mind, Dokja?"

"We need to get out of here," I replied without hesitation.

"G-go out there? Are you crazy?"

"Dokja, I also think that's a bit…"

Even Sangah agreed with Myeongoh this time. *They still don't get it, huh?*

"Then how long do you plan to stay here?"

It was true that my suggestion must've sounded illogical. After all, the area around our train was crawling with monsters.

But I knew that we needed to leave.

"Aren't you worried about your parents? Do you think they're safe with all this going on?"

"I-I've been trying to call them, but the lines are down. Texts won't go through, either."

It seems "parents" was the magic word. Sangah's, Hyeonseong's, and even Myeongoh's faces darkened with concern. Gilyeong stared at the ground without a word. I quietly put my hand on his small shoulder. It was Sangah who broke the silence.

"Let's go. We need to leave."

"N-no! Didn't you hear what that thing said? It told us to take a break. We'll have our heads blown up if we don't do as it said!"

"Let's vote on it."

Sangah put her hand up first, followed by me, then Gilyeong. And that was it.

"…I do want to get back to my unit, but it seems too dangerous to go outside right now. Not to mention the creature's warning."

"Leave if you want! I'm not moving! Not an inch!"

I didn't care about Myeongoh Han, since he'd be useless anyway. The problem was Hyeonseong Lee. I needed to take him with me no matter what.

Then came a loud thud and the sound of crumpling metal. The door connecting our car to car 3707 was starting to get bent out of shape.

"Wh-what was that?"

Myeongoh yelled in panic, but the noise continued.

Wham!

Someone on the other side of the door was trying to break it. My head began to spin at this unexpected situation. *Is it time for the next scenario already? It can't be. The goblin hasn't returned yet. That means…*

I rapidly narrowed down the possibilities, until a chill went down my spine.

It's him.

"Wh-what're you all doing?! Block it!" Myeongoh shouted as he backed away from the door. Hyeonseong moved toward the door, until I stopped him.

"You can't. It's no use."

"What?"

"We need to leave. Now."

I stared at the steel door nervously.

"Huh? But—"

"If we stay here…"

The sole survivor of car 3707. It was painfully obvious who was behind that door.

"…we'll all die before the next scenario even begins."

That's right—he's finally coming. The real "main character" of this story.

3

I looked directly at Hyeonseong and Myeongoh, who were still hesitating.

"Get killed by whoever's behind that door, or try your luck outside this subway. Which do you choose?"

"U-ugh…"

"But, Dokja, how can you be so sure the person in the other car is a threat to us?"

Steel Blade Hyeonseong Lee has a tendency to falter at crucial moments. There's a reason why he's not suited to being a leader.

"They must be a survivor, too. So why don't we meet with—?"

In place of an answer, I looked around at the blood-covered subway car. Hyeonseong followed my gaze, then grew quiet.

"…Never mind. I'll look for a way out."

"L-let's go! We need to get out of here!"

Hyeonseong and Myeongoh had realized it, too. The survivors of other cars must've experienced the same scenario we had. And it was unlikely that they'd all been fortunate enough to have bugs to kill.

"The door's broken!"

"Damn it! This one's stuck, too!"

As Hyeonseong and Myeongoh yelled with growing alarm, I also checked a door. There had been a barrier around the doors earlier, but we could touch them now.

Not counting the doors between cars, each train car had eight exits. And there were three left that we hadn't checked yet.

Bam!

That door wouldn't hold for more than another minute. Even if he was the main character, his strength stat wouldn't be that high near the beginning of the novel. And yet, he was trying to break through a steel door. I couldn't help but feel amazed.

"Dokja! Over here!"

We'd found a manual mechanism that wasn't broken.

"It's opening!"

But even though the wheel turned smoothly, the door didn't open all the way. It got stuck about a fifth of the way.

"...Looks like this one's broken, too."

"How about others?"

"No good. This was our best shot."

The gap was too narrow for anyone other than a small child. Myeongoh and Hyeonseong each grabbed a sliding door and pulled, but it didn't budge.

[Coins Owned: 4,700C]

Coins could be used to increase overall stats. And I'd already spent 2,700 coins to increase my stamina to level 10. I could use the rest to increase my strength, but it'd be risky to use them up at this point. Anything could happen this early in the scenarios, and I might need the coins.

In the end, I had no other choice.

"Hyeonseong, use your skill."

"Huh? What do you mean, my skill...?"

I quietly activated "Character Profile."

[Exclusive skill "Character Profile" has been activated.]

* * *

<Character Profile>
Name: Hyeonseong Lee
Age: 28
Sponsoring Constellation: Master of Steel
Exclusive Attribute: A soldier who turned a blind eye to injustice [Common]
Exclusive Skills: [Bayonet Lv.2], [Camouflage Lv.1], [Patience Lv.1], [Sense of Justice Lv.1]
Stigma: [Great Mountain Push Lv.1]
Total Stats: [Stamina Lv.8], [Strength Lv.8], [Agility Lv.7], [Magic Power Lv.5]
Summary: He has great stats overall. He was chosen by a constellation despite staying silent in the face of injustice. This will lead him to another opportunity.

* * *

I could view Hyeonseong's information without any restrictions. Luckily, he had the same sponsor and attribute as I'd read in the novel.

"You saw your skills when you opened the attribute menu, right? You're a soldier, so there might be something in your kit that can help us in this situation."

"There is... But how do I use it...?"

"Think of yourself using the skill."

"...That's it?"

"Yes, that's how it works. I tried it earlier."

Hyeonseong appeared doubtful for a moment, but seemed to make up his mind and took a deep breath.

"Raaaaaah!"

As he gripped the door, his already-large biceps grew even bigger, almost ripping his shirt sleeves. It looked like he had activated "Great Mountain Push" without issue.

To be exact, "Great Mountain Push" was a not a skill, but a stigma, a power that is granted by a sponsoring constellation. I'd used the more generic term "skill" to avoid suspicion.

Drrrr.

There was a sound like large gears being turned, then the door finally began to open.

"Whoa! It's like he's some kinda superhero!"

"It worked! It really worked!"

[Character *Hyeonseong Lee* has begun to trust you.]
[Your understanding of character *Hyeonseong Lee* has increased.]

He's grown more trustful of me, rather than suspicious. He really is a simple guy.

"Let's get out, quick!"

Still, it was too early to relax. I lifted Gilyeong and handed him to Hyeonseong.

"Hyeonseong, carry the boy on your back."

"Got it."

The steel door to car 3707 will break open soon. But if I'm right, that's not the problem anymore.

...Aw man, I thought this might happen. Didn't I tell you to stay put? Damn it! I'm not done setting up the next scenario.

The angry-looking goblin was floating in the middle of Dongho Bridge.

"Aaah! I told you! We should've stayed put!"

Myeongoh clutched his head, expecting it to explode at any moment. But there was no need for him to do so...

Haah... Well, it can't be helped. I hope you realize how lucky you are!

...because the second scenario began as soon as the subway door was opened.

[The second scenario has begun.]

* * *

<Sub Scenario - Escape>
Category: Sub
Difficulty: E
Mission: Cross the collapsed bridge to reach Oksu Station.
Time Limit: 20 minutes
Reward: 200 coins
Penalty for Failure: ???

* * *

"Dokja, something's not right. It says the 'collapsed bridge,' but the bridge looks fine…"

"Never mind that and just run! Hurry!"

"Oh, okay!"

Actually, Sangah was correct. The bridge hadn't collapsed yet.

In other words, the bridge is bound to collapse soon.

"Dokja, let's go."

"I'm coming."

The reason it was still intact was because we'd left the train before we were supposed to. The goblin had needed ten minutes to prepare. We'd escaped three minutes before that.

You could say we were cheating, but this was the only way we could clear this scenario. Especially since we had someone who was not physically strong.

"Huff… Huff… Hyeonseong has amazing stamina. Must be the army training," Sangah said in amazement as she ran beside me.

"…Save your breath. There's still a long way to go."

Hyeonseong ran at the head of the group with the boy on his back. Not surprising, since he was a monster whose total stats for strength, stamina, and agility added up to twenty-three even without his having invested coins on them.

Behind him was Myeongoh, who was struggling to keep up, then Sangah and me bringing up the rear. It'd be close, but we could make it at this pace.

"Ack! What's that?"

At that moment, Myeongoh screamed. Suddenly, there was massive whirlpool in the middle of the Han River spraying water in every direction.

A gargantuan creature rose from the center of it.

An angler dragon.

The problem was that this one was at least double the size of the one we'd seen from the train. Judging by its size, it wasn't a sea serpent, but a sea commander.

Even sea serpents, the regular variety of angler dragons, were level-7 monsters. Ground rats, level-9 monsters, were a threat to the average person, so anything level 7 or above could kill a human like one would squash a bug.

In other words, the monster swimming toward us was far beyond what anyone could handle this early on in the scenarios. Of course, there was no need for us to fight it. It wasn't meant to be fought.

Splaaaaash!

Huge waves crashed into the bridge, and the angler dragon opened its mouth. It was trying to destroy the bridge by biting through the whole thing.

"It's gonna wreck the bridge!"

"Run! We can make it if we keep running!"

About two hundred meters left to go. At the speed we were going, we would be able to make it before the bridge came down.

Playing the game on easy mode? Where's the fun in that?!

That is, if there weren't any surprises.

[The difficulty of the scenario has been adjusted.]
[Difficulty: E -> D]

I had a sinking feeling. The goblin chuckled.

You're just gonna run? Boring! Let's change things up.

[The spirits of the dead rise up.]
[Black aether surges from the ground.]
[Demonic beings have awoken!]

There was a groaning noise behind us. We were being chased. Sangah glanced over her shoulder and went pale.

"Zombies?"

A horde of zombie-like corpses was swarming toward us. I spotted a few of the other passengers from our train car in their midst.

"We're almost there! Hurry!"

The distance to the angler dragon was less than a hundred meters. Thankfully, Hyeonseong made it to safety with Gilyeong. The problem was the rest of us—including me. Myeongoh screamed, "Bastards! Get away from me!"

There were too many demonic beings coming after us. If it had only been the dead from the subway, we could've run away from them. The problem was...

"Gwuuuh!"

...people who had been in the cars on the bridge had also reanimated.

The area Hyeonseong had crossed earlier was now filled with demonic beings, their eyes aglow with bluish flames. I looked back and forth between the demonic beings blocking our way and the angler dragon drawing closer to us.

"...Everyone, get down."

But it was too late.

—*Craaash!*

The bridge shook violently as the colossal angler dragon bit right through it. Its scales glistened in the cloud of dust, then the water of the Han River rained down. The stench of blood mingled with the fishy smell of river water.

I staggered to my feet. The dust settled, and I surveyed the damage.

Crushed steel frames and piles of concrete rubble. The angler dragon had chomped through a large swathe of demonic beings, leaving pieces of them strewn everywhere.

The bridge had been cut off.

"...Dok...! ...okay?"

Sangah was standing some distance away from me, holding up Myeongoh, with his arm around her shoulder. Myeongoh appeared to have injured his leg and was having trouble walking.

Hyeonseong and Gilyeong were yelling something from across the collapsed section of the bridge, but I couldn't hear them. They were in the safe zone, which was on the other side of a barrier.

What should I do now?

I had considered the possibility of the bridge being destroyed. But I hadn't factored in Myeongoh and Sangah also being here. My thoughts were cut short by a voice ringing through the air.

[Someone has received a constellation's blessing.]
[The constellation's blessing has activated Deus Ex Machina for this scenario.]

With that, a bridge of light appeared spanning the collapsed section of Dongho Bridge. Then a message window came up.

[Deus Ex Machina - The Bridge of Even Numbers]
Explanation: A bridge of light made by a constellation's blessing. Only an even number of people can cross it. If an odd number of people attempt to cross, the bridge of light will disappear immediately.

* * *

"Dokja, uh...in my head, this thing suddenly—"

Sangah was looking at me in confusion. I had a pretty good idea of what was happening.

Deus Ex Machina.

A power that can be used by constellations to directly intervene in a scenario, albeit at a massive cost.

"...It's your sponsor, Sangah."

I didn't know which one it was, but a constellation had chosen Sangah as their incarnation, and they wanted her to live.

Deus Ex Machina is a rare event that only happened a few times in all of *TWSA*.

Not to mention, in the original story, Sangah would've died. I was suddenly curious. Who on earth could her sponsor be?

> [This character's information cannot be viewed via "Character Profile."]
> [This person is not registered in "Character Profile."]

That surprised me. *I can't see her info with my skill? Why not? Is her sponsoring constellation that special? Or does she have the "Mental Barrier" skill? But there's no way she'd have something like that this early... No, wait. Could it be?*

"Dokja, what should we do now?"

Sangah sounded panicked. There was no time to think.

Rumble.

The river was churning below us. I could see the giant angler dragon that had destroyed the bridge turning toward us once again. I bit my lip and read the explanation again.

> Only an even number of people can cross it.

Deus Ex Machina was devised by constellations, those sadistic bastards who love tragedy.

There was no outcome where everyone would survive.

Myeongoh shuddered as our eyes met.

Someone had to die.

4

At that moment, Sangah yelled, "Dokja! Behind you!"

I ducked instinctively, barely dodging a bloody fist. A familiar fist, wrapped in a dark aura.

I reflexively kicked backward as I fell forward, and felt it connect. Even without looking, I had a hunch who it was.

A level-9 humanoid—demonic being.

A human infected by black aether.

Despite being level 9, they are considered highly dangerous. Normal humans who become demonic beings are little more than zombies, but depending on the host, they can be extremely threatening…like this one.

I looked at the name tag on the headless body's school uniform.

"…Namwoon Kim."

The high school boy whose head had exploded ten minutes ago. He'd been reanimated as a demonic being, and I was his target.

Namwoon's exposed vocal cords writhed grotesquely.

"Guhh."

> [Exclusive skill "Omniscient Reader's Viewpoint" has been activated.]
> [The target is not sentient. "Omniscient Reader's Viewpoint" is canceled.]

Damn, it doesn't work?

Shhk!

Namwoon's nails, which had grown into long, black claws, slashed my thigh. A burning pain spread through my whole leg. He hadn't been able to cut through my skin with a knife before, but now he could do it with his bare hands. Demonic beings become many times stronger than they were as humans.

"Sangah, we have to—"

I was about to talk to my companions when I got a sinking feeling. I didn't have to turn around to see what was happening.

"Let go! Let go of me! Dokja! Dokja…!"

Myeongoh Han, who had been limping not too long ago, was zooming across the bridge at an incredible speed while carrying Sangah.

[Constellation *Secretive Plotter* is amazed by how gullible you are.]
[Constellation *Demonic Judge of Fire* is touched by your selflessness.]
[You have received 100 coins as a donation.]

……I see how it is.

I'd been abandoned.

The way Myeongoh was running was quite strange. Despite only using one leg, he was going as fast as an Olympic runner. There was no way an out-of-shape middle-aged man like him would have such a skill, so it had to be his sponsoring constellation's stigma.

[One-Legged Swift Foot]

I knew which constellation provided that stigma. I used "Character Profile" on Myeongoh as he ran farther from me.

[This character's information cannot be viewed via "Character Profile."]

Again. It didn't work.

If I remembered correctly, "One-Legged Swift Foot" was a stigma of Limping Trickster. That constellation didn't grant any mental barrier stigma. And there was no way Myeongoh had that kind of skill on his own.

In other words, the reason my skill wasn't working on him had nothing to do with any of his abilities.

...How stupid of me.

Looking at the message in front of me, I let out a wry chuckle.

[This person is not registered in "Character Profile."]

I'd been overthinking it, instead of taking those words at face value. "Character Profile" is a skill that displays a character's information. And Sangah Yu and Myeongoh Han were not characters from *TWSA*.

If I hadn't saved them, they'd be dead. No wonder I couldn't find their information in "Character Profile."

"Grrr! Grrr! Grrr!"

On one side, Namwoon Kim and the other demonic beings were shuffling toward me, groaning unintelligibly. In the other direction, Myeongoh had made it halfway across the bridge. Since Hyeonseong and Gilyeong were already in the safe zone, they couldn't help me. In other words, I'd been left high and dry.

I had to think quickly. Subdue one of the demonic beings and cross with it? It might have been worth trying, but I didn't like my chances. These monsters may have been classified as humanoids, but they weren't actually humans, meaning they might not satisfy the condition for crossing the bridge of light.

"Groar!"

Some of the demonic beings lunged at me but lost their footing and fell off the bridge.

Crunch!

They instantly became food for the angler dragons. The serpentine monsters swarmed like piranhas in a feeding frenzy, scattering bits and pieces of the demonic beings in the water.

Icy tendrils of fear crept down my spine. If I tried to cross the bridge alone, making an odd number, I'd meet the same fate. So that wasn't an option. Then what?

"......Slow down. Think."

I muttered to myself, trying to calm my nerves. I needed to stay rational. There were still a few things I could try, but first, I had to deal with the enemies in front of me. I controlled my breathing and focused on tripping the demonic beings that lunged at me.

"Guhh?"

Luckily, they didn't have eyes, so it was easy to use their own momentum to make them fall off the edge.

Kraaah—! Crunch!

I was steadily thinning their numbers. The goblin's timer began to blink.

Fifteen minutes remaining until the scenario ends.

"Haah..."

There was a gash on my shoulder from an attack that had come from my blind spot. No matter how much information I had, my body was fragile and untrained.

"Groar!"

There was nothing left of Namwoon's mind except feral instinct. His attacks grew faster and faster.

Left shoulder.

Right thigh.

Head.

I needed to break his flow. I stomped hard on his leg as I barely dodged his claws.

"Graah?"

But he no longer had a sense of pain, so my attack did little to impede his advance. I staggered backward until I felt exposed metal beams underfoot. I could hear the angler dragons below thrashing in anticipation as they saw me teetering on the edge.

[A small number of constellations are entertained by your struggle.]
[A small number of constellations have donated 200 coins.]

The coins were racking up. I had over five thousand at this point. A hefty sum for the early stages of the scenario.

Wow! He's holding up pretty well, isn't he? Now! Is there any constellation willing to bestow their blessing upon this poor incarnation?

The goblin sounded like an auctioneer.

I wished I could tear its smug face apart.

Going once! Going twice...! Seriously? No one...?

Of course there was no one. It'd be strange for any constellation to support me now, considering the choice I'd made during Sponsor Selection.

And that's why you should've taken the help when it was offered. What a pity.

I failed to dodge Namwoon's attack and took a hit to my waist. Of course, I'd been fighting back the best I could, too. I'd torn up the left side of his torso and shoulder with a knife. His intestines were spilling out of the gaping wound, bouncing like jump rope.

In order to kill a demonic being, you have to crush its heart.

However, the skin around its heart is the toughest, so a Swiss Army knife wasn't enough to pierce through.

Damn it, if I only had a combat skill, this would be easier.

[Exclusive skill "Bookmark" has been activated.]

...Bookmark?

["Character Bookmark" has been activated.]
[Available bookmark slots: 3]
[Loading the list of bookmarks available for activation.]

* * *

<List of Bookmarked Characters>
1. Delusional Demon Namwoon Kim [Understanding 25]
2. Steel Blade Hyeonseong Lee [Understanding 35]
3. Empty slot

* * *

"Bookmark." I'd read three thousand chapters of *TWSA* but had never seen this skill before. Yet I instinctively knew how to use it.

"Activate the first bookmark."

I felt a fluttering sensation as pages of a book flipped by in my head. They were scenes from *TWSA* with Namwoon Kim.

Gah-ha-ha-ha! I'm so freaking strong!
Die! Die! Die! Die!
A new world needs new rules.

As his memories flooded into my head, every muscle and nerve in my body tensed up. The unfamiliar power of someone other than me was surging within me.

[The first bookmark has been activated.]
[Duration is shortened because your "Bookmark" skill level is low.]
[Duration: 1 minute]

One minute. That's more than enough.

[The character's skill will only be partially effective due to your low understanding of this character.]
["Dark Awakening" Lv.1 has been activated.]

Breathing raggedly, Namwoon lunged at me. The black aether surrounding him threatened to burst forth and engulf me. I focused as much energy as I could in my heels. Then I dashed headlong at Namwoon.

If I had the same skill as him, I wouldn't lose.

I really was Namwoon Kim himself at that moment. The unhinged murderer who, along with the main character, had struck fear into the world of *TWSA*. The Delusional Demon who could take on any foe once his Dark Awakening was activated.

"Kraaaah!"

I felt the sickening sensation of sinew and flesh being torn as the Swiss Army knife in my hand ripped through his body, from left shoulder all the way to the heart. The demonic being that had once been Namwoon Kim staggered as its body was torn apart.

If he had eyes, he would've been looking at me.

"Guhh…I…grrr…don't…"

The cynical young man who had dreamed of rebelling against the world he despised. Had the story of *TWSA* never happened, he might have taken the entrance exam, entered a university, and enjoyed campus life, just like a normal person.

"...don't...wanna...die..."

I regarded him wordlessly as he careened off the railing. I'd hated his character, but at that moment, I was seized with inexplicable sorrow.

[Your understanding of character *Namwoon Kim* has increased.]
[The first bookmark has been deactivated.]

A tidal wave of emptiness and fatigue crashed over me.

I was exhausted.

"Groar!"

I had ten minutes remaining. There was still a sizable swarm of demonic beings shuffling toward me. Far too many for someone with only level-10 stamina to deal with. But it had never been my intention to deal with them alone.

...He's a bit late. It's about time he appeared.

Crunch! Snap!

As if on cue, there was the sound of flesh and bone being crushed. I knew it. That guy would definitely pull a stunt like this if it meant raking in more donations and achievements.

Crack! Crunch!

Even though it was a living human tearing through the bodies of what used to be humans, it sounded like an iron mace slamming down on flesh.

To be honest, I'd thought I might stand a chance against the main character with the number of coins I'd amassed. But watching the carnage unfolding in front of my eyes, I realized how sorely mistaken I'd been.

From the spot he'd left the train, there was a straight line of demonic beings' broken bodies, like a trail left by a tank charging through dense foliage. Was it even possible for a human to cause such devastation?

"Graah?"

Even the headless abominations noticed something was off and turned toward the commotion one by one. But it was too late.

Craaack!

In the blink of an eye, the man smashed every demonic being in his way and stood before me. Here was a force of nature that had torn through a horde of enemies with his bare hands.

I thought I'd steeled myself for this moment, but I felt cold sweat dripping down my back. Fight a monster like him? There was no chance. Even if my stats were double what they were now, I couldn't win against him.

"Who are you?"

The man's cold gaze fell on me. I activated "Character Profile" to fight off the fear.

[Exclusive skill "Character Profile" has been activated.]
[There is too much information about this character. Switching to a summarized view.]

* * *

Name: Junghyeok Yu
Attributes: Regressor, <Third Loop> [Mythical], Pro Gamer [Rare]
Exclusive Skills: [The Eye of the Sage Lv.8], [Close Combat Lv.8], [Weapon Proficiency Lv.8], [Mental Barrier Lv.5], [Crowd Control Lv.5], [Reasoning Lv.5], [Lie Detection Lv.4]...

* * *

The list of skills went on and on. From near the bottom of the list, a powerful hand shot out and gripped my neck.

"How the hell are you still alive?"

The first way to survive the apocalypse. This man standing in front of me was the living embodiment of that.

The Regressor Junghyeok Yu.

The endless tragedies of this world all begin with this character.

5

A grown man held up by the neck and dangling in the air like a monkey. It must've been quite a comical scene.

I could see my companions looking in my direction from the other side of the bridge. They seemed concerned, but they wouldn't actually know what was happening to me. The barrier was like a one-way mirror—I could see them, but they couldn't see me.

"Name."

"Huh?"

"What's your name?"

How rude. *Typical main character.* But I shouldn't provoke him now.

"I'm Dokja Kim."

"What a weird name."

"I get that a lot—"

Suddenly, my stomach caved in, and I nearly vomited. Junghyeok Yu's fist was buried underneath my solar plexus.

"...Urgh."

My skin was hard enough to repel a knife blade, but his punch hurt quite a lot.

"A tough body. You already know how to use coins, don't you?"

"So do y—"

Wham. My insides buckled from another blow. I barely stopped myself from groaning in pain.

This guy's strength must have been at least level 15. After just one main and one sub scenario, he was already this strong. *He's just built different.*

"You talk too much. You will speak only when I ask you a question, understood?"

I didn't answer. I'd figured I might find myself in this situation. But this was the worst possible outcome I'd been trying to avoid.

Early on, Junghyeok Yu was more dangerous than anyone else.

Going through three regressions had eroded his humanity. In order to manage his enlarged ego, he'd come up with certain principles he followed closely. Junghyeok Yu would not hesitate to do whatever it took to achieve his goals.

"Your answer?"

"...Fine."

"I don't like your tone."

"Deal with it."

This time, I raised my arms to block his fist. It hurt like every bone in my hands had broken, but it lessened the impact of his punch. Junghyeok's eyes widened with surprise.

[Character *Junghyeok Yu* is wary of you.]

That's right. You might be the main character, but that doesn't mean I'll stand here and let you beat me up.

"Sorry, but I'm older than you, pro gamer Junghyeok Yu. So *you* watch *your* tone."

"...You know who I am?"

"Yeah. I worked at a game company."

Of course, that was a lie. Well, it was true that I'd worked at Mino Soft, but that didn't mean I'd memorized the name of every pro gamer. Not only that, but until a few hours ago, Junghyeok Yu was nothing but a novel character to me.

"You're famous in that scene, you know? I used to be a fan."

His being famous was just a part of his backstory. But I wasn't lying when I said I was a fan.

I'd liked, hated, resented, and rooted for Junghyeok Yu.

He and I had gone through three thousand chapters of the story together.

"A fan? Haven't heard that in a while."

Junghyeok seemed to reminisce about the past. But only for a brief moment.

"I'll forgive you for being rude. But that doesn't change anything."

"Yeah, I can see that."

I looked down and saw my legs dangling in the air.

"There's only one thing I want to ask you."

"Go ahead."

"How did you survive in the subway?"

I knew he'd ask me that.

"Will you let me live if I tell you?"

"Depends."

Bullshit. I could tell just by looking at his face. I wasn't the only reader of *TWSA* for nothing. I ran countless simulations in my head of how I'd answer and how he'd react. What could I say to persuade this regressor jerk?

[Your understanding of character *Junghyeok Yu* has increased.]
[Your understanding of this character is very high.]

...Huh?

[You have met the conditions for using level 2 of the exclusive skill "Omniscient Reader's Viewpoint."]
[Would you like to activate the exclusive skill?]

And just like that, I could read his thoughts as they flooded into my head.

[The only ones who were supposed to survive in that car were Hyeonseong Lee and Namwoon Kim.]

[But Namwoon Kim is dead, and other people made it out instead.]

[How did they survive?]

[Who is this guy?]

[I need more information. And if he turns out to be an obstacle......I'll kill him.]

Junghyeok's thoughts raced by at a dizzying pace. There was nothing funny about my current situation, but I couldn't stop my mouth from curling into a smile.

There were five minutes remaining until the end of the scenario.

I began to tell my story, keeping things simple, short, and accurate. From the moment the goblin appeared in my subway car to the end of the first scenario. Of course, I left out any sensitive details, like what skills I'd obtained.

"...You cleared the scenario by killing bugs?"

"I got lucky."

Junghyeok was so surprised that he didn't notice his own mouth was agape.

[The future has completely changed.]

It must've been shocking indeed.

Car 3807 was supposed to have devolved into a battle royal, with only Namwoon Kim and Hyeonseong Lee surviving.

"That's awfully sharp of you. How did you know there were bugs in that car?"

A murderous glint flashed in his eyes, and my head was flooded with his thoughts.

[Is he also a Regressor?]

[If he is, I have to kill him now.]

Of course that's what he suspects of me. Textbook projection. I quickly replied.

"There was an explosion."

"An explosion?"

"I'm saying I was able to spot the bugs because there was an explosion in the car in front of ours."

Junghyeok perked up at the mention of the other train car.

"Elaborate so I can understand."

"A kid in my car fell down because of the explosion and dropped his bug cage. And I happened to pick it up."

"...What a suspicious coincidence."

"Coincidences are always suspicious. If you don't believe me, ask the people on the other side of that barrier. The boy with the bug cage is there, too."

We could see the people looking at us from beyond the barrier, on the road toward Oksu Station. They couldn't call out or come to us because the scenario was still ongoing.

Junghyeok glanced at them but did not move. All of a sudden, my vision grew blurry and what seemed like Junghyeok's memories flashed before my eycs.

[I see.]
[The explosion.]
[This guy's not a Regressor.]
[The future didn't change because of him. Rather, the reason it changed...]
[...is because of me?]

People screaming in agony as they died from the explosion, and Junghyeok Yu looking at them, devoid of emotion.

[It was because I did something different this time and killed everyone with an explosion right at the beginning.]

It might have been the effect of "Omniscient Reader's Viewpoint," but I could feel every bit of mental anguish that seized Junghyeok.

"Are you done with the questions?"

"...Yes."

"Then can you let go? We should head to Oksu Station together. There isn't much time left."

"I can't do that."

But there's a reason why he's the main character.

"Everything fits too perfectly."

I'd never seen any other main characters more cautious than Junghyeok Yu.

[He's too calm for a beginner.]
[It's uncanny how well he's adapting to the new world.]
[I'm sure he's one who killed Namwoon Kim.]
[He may prove useful, but more importantly, he's dangerous.]

Junghyeok's right eye glowed with a golden light. I realized what he was about to do. Actually, it was odd that he hadn't used it on me already.

"The Eye of the Sage."

Junghyeok Yu's peerless detection skill—an SS-grade skill that allows him to see not only your attribute window, but all your hidden information as well. Once he used it, he'd learn about my identity. But a part of me thought this might be a good thing.

I still didn't know what my own attribute and skills were. Even if it meant having my info laid bare to Junghyeok, it could be a chance for me to find out more about myself as well. I might even be able to use that information to better navigate my current predicament.

[Exclusive skill "The Fourth Wall" has been activated.]
["The Fourth Wall" has identified a detection skill, "The Eye of the Sage"!]

Sparks flew into the air and Junghyeok's body contorted.

[...Kgh! What?]

Junghyeok glared at me with shock and alarm, one hand clamped over his right eye.

"Who… What the hell are you?"
I'm sorry but I'm curious about that, too.

[Exclusive skill "The Fourth Wall" has blocked "The Eye of the Sage."]

……No way. I had a skill that could block "The Eye of the Sage"? "Bookmark," and now "The Fourth Wall"… *This complicates things. He probably doesn't believe me anymore.*

[I have to kill him now.]

He wasn't the type to trust something he didn't understand.
"Junghyeok Yu."
In that case, I had to change my approach.
"You need an ally you can trust."
"…What're you talking about?"
"You know you can't clear the forty-sixth scenario by yourself, right?"
His eyes narrowed.
"How do you know about that? Don't tell me you're—"
"It doesn't matter who I am."
I looked straight into Junghyeok's eyes. "What's important is that I can help you."

[He's not a Regressor. I'd definitely recognize him if he were.]
[Then what is he?]
[…Could he be?]

A game of cards where I couldn't hide my hand or play my best card. Then there was only one thing I could do.
Play a hand that would mislead my opponent.
"Junghyeok, I know the future that you don't know about."

[Character *Junghyeok Yu* has activated the skill "Lie Detection."]
["Lie Detection" has confirmed your words to be true.]

Junghyeok's eyes slowly widened.
"...How?"
"What do you think?"

[It can't be. There's a Prophet other than Anna Croft? In Korea, no less?]

Prophet.
The only attribute in *TWSA* with the ability to see the future. It is also the only attribute that grants the passive effect "Nullify Detection Skill."
In *TWSA*, there is one character who possesses this attribute.

[Only a Prophet can block my skill "The Eye of the Sage."]

I didn't answer. Junghyeok bit his lip.
"Are you saying you can use 'Future Sight'?"
"Something like that."
"Then you must've known I'd come this way."
"That's right."

[I see. If this guy is a Prophet, then all his actions make sense.]

Things were getting turned around. I could feel Junghyeok was agitated. This was my only chance.
"Junghyeok Yu, I know you possess a special power. You also know what will happen in the future, don't you?"
"……"
"But you're also aware that your knowledge is incomplete."

It's the Regressor's only weakness.

The very act of using their foreknowledge to change the present alters the future. In other words, they must eventually face an "unknown future."

"Let me be your ally. I can complement what you lack."

To Junghyeok Yu, there's no better teammate than a Prophet. And I could fulfill a similar role, because I was the only reader of this story.

[One minute remaining until the end of the scenario.]

Junghyeok looked down, lost in thought.

[A Prophet would be helpful indeed.]

[Fifty seconds remaining until the end of the scenario.]

[Not only for the forty-sixth scenario, but also for fighting the Zarathustra bastards later on. But…can I trust him?]

[Forty seconds remaining until the end of the scenario.]

[An ally.]

I was anxiously watching the clock when Junghyeok looked up.

"I've decided. I'll make you my ally."

[You are mentally drained due to excessive concentration.]

[Exclusive skill "Omniscient Reader's Viewpoint" has been deactivated.]

I didn't know if it was my fatigue or relief that caused it, but my skill deactivated at the worst possible time. Suddenly, Junghyeok's face seemed utterly inscrutable to me, like a complex philosophical thesis without any footnotes.

He began crossing the Bridge of Even Numbers with me, still holding me up by the neck...... But all things considered, I thought it had worked out pretty well. I'd actually persuaded this damn regressor. I felt quite proud of myself.

Junghyeok suddenly stopped just outside the safe zone, after having crossed most of the bridge.

"One last question."

"What is it?"

"If you're really a Prophet, then you can see your own future, right?"

The dead calm in his eyes gave me a shudder.

Junghyeok hadn't finished testing me yet. His grip around my neck was suffocating.

"Urk."

He slowly stretched out his arm that was holding me up, then a gust of wind hit my feet. I was hanging over the edge of the bridge. Directly below me was the bloodied Han River. Angler dragons were jumping out of the water, crazed by the sight of a prey dangling above them.

"Tell me, will I let go or not?"

Cold sweat dripped down my back. *Think. I know him better than anyone.* I closed my eyes and thought about the Junghyeok Yu that I knew.

[Twenty seconds remaining until the end of the scenario.]

I came to a conclusion.

"Junghyeok Yu."

This bastard would do it. No matter how I thought about it, the result was the same. I went on, eyeing the sea commander that was swimming toward me.

"Let me make two things clear."

"...What?"

"First, I'm not your lackey. Treat me as an equal."

"......"

"Second, promise that you'll cooperate with me as I will cooperate with you."

A look of amusement flashed in Junghyeok's eyes. He nodded.

"Very well. And your answer is?"

I responded with a smile.

"Let go already, you piece of shit."

And just like that, there was nothing keeping me up anymore. *Ah, so this is what gravity feels like.*

Even as I fell, I could see Junghyeok's face. I didn't know what he was so happy about, but he was smiling radiantly.

Son of a bitch.

"I believe you now. You really are a Prophet."

Waiting at the end of my fall was the sea commander's maw.

A bone-rattling impact, then the cold water of the Han River engulfed me. I barely managed to gasp a mouthful of air before warm, vast darkness swallowed me.

[You have failed to clear the scenario.]

EPISODE

03

The Contract

1

My body grew heavy as my lungs filled with water. I felt myself being swallowed, then sucked down the gullet. At least I'd fallen just so that I didn't get chewed up. But it would all be over if I lost consciousness here.

Stay alert. I just have to hold on a little longer.

I curled up into a ball and desperately held my breath. Ten seconds, twenty seconds, thirty seconds...my hands touched a squishy wall, and I finally allowed myself to gasp.

"U-urgh."

I had to vomit out river water several times before I could breathe normally. Thanks to my level-10 stamina, I'd survived hitting the water's surface, but my whole body ached from scrapes and bruises all over.

Fighting back the panic that threatened to overtake me, I rummaged for my phone. I was scared it might've gotten damaged in the fall, but thankfully, the screen lit up. Good thing I'd shelled out for a waterproof model.

Flash.

I turned on the flashlight and surveyed my surroundings. Chunks of concrete jutted out from the surface of the water, which was littered with floating debris. And all around, towering walls of viscera. The angler dragon's innards were more disgusting than I'd imagined.

"Damn it."

The image of Junghyeok's face as he let go without hesitation was burned into my memory. I'd expected it, but the shock of having actually experienced it was fresh in my mind.

……*"Survive this, if you want to be my ally." I guess that's the gist of it.*

It was understandable, though. Junghyeok, of all people, would not take the word "ally" lightly. Ever since he'd failed his first loop, he'd never taken a true ally.

Most normal humans couldn't possibly keep up with a Regressor. Because of that, he'd been forced to take care of everything by himself. People looked up to him as the savior, and naturally, he'd grown lonely. To him, other humans were either followers or enemies.

That was why he was testing me. If I couldn't get through this on my own, he wouldn't see me as an equal…… That must have been his reasoning, at least.

"Ally my ass…… You absolute psychopath."

I dog-paddled to a foam panel and barely pulled myself up. The warmth of the angler dragon's insides had thawed my body, but the real problem was what I'd do from here on. I replayed the message log I'd heard as I fell.

[You have failed to clear the scenario.]
[Proceeding to checkout.]
[100 coins were deducted for channel usage.]
[Constellation *Prisoner of the Golden Headband* nods in approval of your bold words.]
[You have received 100 coins as a donation.]
[Constellation *Demonic Judge of Fire* nods in approval of your decision.]
[You have received 100 coins as a donation.]
[Constellation *Secretive Plotter* is disappointed by your imprudent words.]

There were quite a lot of messages. The donations from the constellations who had revealed their epithets stood out. Must have been because of the last conversation I'd had with Junghyeok. Going through each message and collecting my earnings, I felt a pang of regret. Maybe if I'd chosen one of those constellations, I wouldn't have ended up like this.

But there was no looking back. Having met Junghyeok Yu face-to-face, it had become clear. Although the Great Sage, Heaven's Equal was a top-tier constellation, he alone wouldn't be enough. I needed something more than a sponsoring constellation to go up against Junghyeok. And this would be the first step to getting that.

Slosh. The angler dragon's stomach undulated, causing a small wave. The sea commander must have been swimming somewhere. I turned on my phone and calculated the time.

According to *TWSA*, angler dragons start secreting stomach acid three hours after a meal. In other words, I didn't have much time.

Ha-ha. What a shame. You were putting on such a good show.

There was a crackling sound, and a voice echoed in the damp air.

"…Goblin?"

That's right. You don't seem surprised at all.

"Because I knew you'd come."

Hmm, so you've been waiting for me.

"Of course."

A flash of light, and the goblin appeared in midair. I couldn't tell what was going through the creature's head, but it was clearly intrigued. I tried my best to sound casual. *I have to take the lead here, or it will all be for nothing.*

"You have some coins to collect from me, don't you?"

......Coins?

"I failed the scenario, so I have to pay the penalty."

Hmm, don't you mean your life?

"If that were the case, it would've said 'Death' as the penalty for failure instead of three question marks. It means there's room for negotiation, no?"

...Ha-ha-ha. Interesting.

Actually, what I'd said wasn't completely correct. "Penalty for Failure: ???" in the scenario message meant just that—the penalty was unknown.

It was a leap of logic to assume that the penalty was coins. Even so, I was confident.

"Am I wrong?"

Because I already knew about this scenario.

The goblin hesitated for moment, then nodded.

You're right. You figured out all that based on one tiny clue...? No wonder the constellations have their eyes on you.

The goblin sounded genuinely impressed.

As you said, you can survive even if you fail a sub scenario, as long as you have enough coins.

"How much?"

Pay me 5,100 coins. Then I'll let you live.

I checked my balance.

[Coins Owned: 5,100C]

I scoffed. *So this is how you want to play it, huh?*

"That's too much."

Ha-ha. Then have fun dying. Taking coins instead of your life is entirely at my discretion. I can end you anytime I want.

"Go right ahead."

......What?

"I said, kill me."

......

"You can't, can you?"

The goblin didn't do anything. Of course it didn't. I was the money-maker for its channel. Besides, it wouldn't have come all the way here to chat if it meant to kill me off. This creature had every reason to want me to make a miraculous comeback here, or at least die in the most spectacular, agonizing way possible.

Ha-ha. You're starting to piss me off. Look, do you really think I—

The goblin's eyebrow twitched with annoyance. *Time to stop provoking it and get to the main point.*

"Low-grade goblin Bihyeong. How's being a streamer working out for you?"

The goblin froze almost like a cartoon. For the first time, its smug face was seized with panic.

...Wh-what? How do you know my name?

"Streaming isn't so hot these days, huh? Must be hard when the constellations are so stingy with coins."

Wh-who the hell are you? How can a mere human know about—?!

Bihyeong's horns quivered. Its shock was understandable. A normal human couldn't possibly know anything about the Star Stream System.

But I'm not a normal human.

[A small number of constellations have become suspicious about your identity.]
[Constellation ***Secretive Plotter***'s eyes glint in anticipation of your devious plan.]

It wouldn't be good for constellations to hear what I was about to say. I only mouthed my words to Bihyeong.

"Why don't you shut off your channel for a bit so we can continue this conversation?"

Bihyeong looked torn for a few seconds, then shut off his channel.

[Channel #BI-7623 is offline.]

Once the constellations were gone, the goblin dropped all pretense.

Now tell me. How do you, a mere human, know about Star Stream?

"That's not important."

Huh?

"Bihyeong, don't you want to be the Goblin King?"

What are you—?

"Forget Dokak or Gildal. I'm talking the best goblin storyteller there ever was."

The expression on Bihyeong's face was changing.

"Goblin Bihyeong, make a contract with me. Then I will make you the Goblin King."

2

Star Stream System.

Simply put, Star Stream is a broadcast system aimed at the entire universe.

Constellations sitting atop faraway galaxies are its audience. Humans like me are the actors. And connecting the two as the storytellers are the goblins just like the one before my eyes.

Ha...ha-ha-ha-ha-ha! You're crazy! Completely insane! I should've realized when you turned down all the offers during Sponsor Selection!

Bihyeong laughed for a while, then continued.

I'm not sure how you know about Star Stream, but I can't accept your proposal. You see, I'm a goblin, not a constellation, so I can't become your sponsor.

"I think you misunderstood. I'm not asking you to sponsor me."

Huh?

"I know you're nothing but a weak, bottom-level goblin. I don't need your power. I just need your channel."

My channel?

"Do you not understand? Is your Korean language patch not complete?"

Look here, you—

"I'll make it simple. I want to sign an exclusive contract with your channel."

Bihyeong's face went blank, as if he couldn't process what I'd just said. Then he blinked.

Wait. Are you saying you want to make a stream contract with me?

"That's right."

Normally, a stream contract is an agreement between goblins and constellations. The constellations have their incarnations appear on the goblin's channel. In return, the goblin receives a share of the coins earned by the incarnation as a commission. Normally, the incarnation doesn't get a say in any of this. After all, they're little more than slaves to their sponsors.

Ha-ha. That's rich.

Bihyeong covered his eyes with his tiny hands and laughed. The air around him began to change.

I don't know where you heard about all this, but learn your place. A human proposing a stream contract? You're nothing but an insect who doesn't even have a sponsor!

A simple change in the goblin's tone was enough to fill the surrounding atmosphere with murderous intent. Even a low-grade goblin is incomparably more powerful than a human, after all. But if something like that was enough to make me back down, I wouldn't have started this in the first place.

"It's precisely because I don't have a sponsor that this is a good deal for you."

......Huh?

"Why do you think constellations watch these channels in the first place?"

Bihyeong was caught off guard by my unexpected question. He floated there with his mouth agape, like a bad student who had been called on by the professor. *Time for a special lecture for this low-grade goblin.*

"Relax, you already know all this. But it can't hurt to review, right?"

With that, I was in the driver's seat. Bihyeong was actually nodding along to my words without realizing.

"The subscribers of Star Stream can be divided into two broad categories. First, 'thrill seekers' who flip through channels to pass the time. And second, 'incarnation seekers' who are searching for people to sponsor."

Yes, that's right.

"For your channel to succeed, you need to satisfy at least one of those groups. You either provide good entertainment or suitable candidates to sponsor."

You know your stuff, I admit, but what does any of this have to do with you?

"You still don't get it? No wonder your subscriber count is stuck at three digits."

...Shaddup. Just get to the point!

Bihyeong pointed his little horns at me in frustration. I found it hard to believe this cute ball of fur had been blowing up people's heads just a short while ago.

Anyway, I'd better stop teasing him and get to the point.

"What if there was a channel that satisfied both 'thrill seekers' and 'incarnation seekers'?"

Nonsense! That's not possible. Well, maybe it is, but not for long.

Bihyeong was correct. The very nature of "incarnation seekers" meant it was impossible to keep them interested on a long-term basis.

Constellations who only wanted to find incarnations would change the channel once Sponsor Selection was over, even if there were interesting humans.

In other words, their viewership was temporary. However...

"That's only if Sponsor Selection plays out as it typically does."

Huh?

"But what if there's an incarnation who won't select a sponsor? And that incarnation far surpasses others despite not having a sponsor?"

Strong incarnations drew attention from constellations simply by existing. But if that incarnation didn't select a sponsor, "incarnation seekers" would find it hard to leave the channel.

N-no way. That's why you didn't choose a sponsor...?

"That's right."

Haah... How interesting.

Bihyeong laughed as if this was the most ridiculous thing he'd ever heard.

The most powerful incarnation, without a sponsoring constellation... If there was such a being, the channel featuring them would indeed shoot up to the top of Star Stream. But that's simply not possible.

"Do you really think so?"

......I admit you're no average human. You grabbed the constellations' attention from the very start, and I made bank thanks to that. But now you're being delusional. Haven't the recent events taught you anything? An ordinary human can never beat an incarnation with a sponsor. That's the law of this world.

"You don't know that yet."

You had your chance, and you lost it. Just look at yourself. You failed a scenario. A sub scenario, not even a main one. And now, you're about to die. No constellation would be interested in a failure like y—

"Are you sure about that?"

......?

"Your viewers are throwing a fit right now, aren't they? They're clamoring for you to open the channel back up."

Bihyeong was silent.

"I bet they're dying to know. 'Who's the crazy bastard who went up against the Regressor himself?' 'Can he really see the future?' 'If he can, then why did he get eaten by the angler dragon?'"

St-stop! What are you...?

"I'm telling you it's possible, and I'll show you. All you need to do is shut up and do as I say. And I'll make you the Goblin King!"

Bihyeong was looking at me differently. He gulped audibly. I could almost hear the gears turning in his head. He had nothing to lose by trusting me. His eyes darted around rapidly.

First things first, pay up for failing the scenario. If you give me 5,100 coins—

"What're you talking about? I didn't fail."

......Huh?

"I'm sure that by now, the conditions have been met…"

I stood up and stretched. Joints all over my body cracked in protest. Bihyeong still had a dumbfounded expression on his face.

"Just open the channel. It's about to start."

Start? What's—?

Then a message rang out from thin air.

[A hidden scenario has been unlocked!]

<Hidden Scenario - Commander Slayer>
Category: Hidden
Difficulty: A+
Mission: Slay the angler dragon "sea commander," and escape from its stomach.
Time Limit: 10 days
Reward: 9,000 coins
Penalty for Failure: Death

* * *

"I told you to get ready."

There are three kinds of scenarios in *TWSA*.

Main scenarios progress the overarching story.

Sub scenarios are about small events that fill in the gaps in the narrative.

And hidden scenarios are only unlocked when special conditions are met.

What? I can't... How do you know things even I haven't heard about...?

Bihyeong's face was contorted in astonishment. His lips quivered. Unlike main and sub scenarios, hidden scenarios only activate when specific conditions are met.

"It's not surprising that you didn't know. You're a low-grade goblin, after all."

Wh-what are you?

"Anyway, if I clear this, that should be enough proof I have what it takes to make a contract with you, right?"

For some reason, Bihyeong looked glum as he stared at the scenario message. He then turned to me with a look of concern.

This scenario's difficulty is A+, you know? Do you really believe you can clear this?

"That's right."

River water sloshed into the angler dragon's stomach lining. When the waves calmed, Bihyeong spoke again.

...Fine. If you can pull this off, we have a deal.

"We'll discuss the terms after I clear the scenario."

You cocky piece of— Well, I'm gonna open the channel again, so good luck.

"Oh, wait."

I couldn't have him leave yet. I had something to check.

"There's one more thing I need from you."

......What now?

Bihyeong sounded annoyed.

"Fix the system error I keep getting."

System error?

"I can't open my attribute menu."

No way. The system doesn't make errors. The scenario system is perfect.

"Look at it and tell me that again."

Bihyeong stared at me incredulously, then began mumbling to the air.

[Goblin *Bihyeong* is attempting to use "System Interference" on you.]

"System Interference." An absolute interference skill only goblins can use.

To be honest, it wasn't clear if an error was the cause of my inability to see my own attribute menu. But I was sure a goblin would figure something out. And even if it couldn't, that in itself could be a clue.

[Exclusive skill "The Fourth Wall" has been activated!]

Sparks flew through the air, and Bihyeong yelped in surprise.

3

Judging by his reaction, I could see it wasn't going as expected.

"Is there a problem?"

This can't be right. There shouldn't be anything that can block "System Interference"...

It looked like "The Fourth Wall" was able to block the interference of not only incarnations, but also goblins. That meant no one, including me, could see my attribute menu.

Interesting.

I had the perfect setup to become a con man.

"If you can't do it, never mind."

W-wait! I should be able to— Argh. What if I try this?

"I said, it's fine."

Gyaaagh!

Bihyeong had apparently touched something he wasn't supposed to, and screamed like he had suffered a nasty shock. His fluffy white fur was singed black.

Th-this thing! It just—

"Enough of that. Forget about it and just do me a favor."

I can't stop here. I'm Bihyeong the goblin. On my goblin's honor, I must solve this—

I looked at the clock. It had been an hour since I'd been swallowed by the angler dragon. There was no time to waste.

"Goblin Shop."

Bihyeong stopped flailing in the air.

What?

"Open the Goblin Shop."

......How do you also know about that?

"Are you going to open it or not?"

An incarnation without a sponsoring constellation can't use—

"Yes, all the incarnations who use the Goblin Shop happen to have sponsoring constellations. But there's no rule that an incarnation without a sponsoring constellation can't use the shop."

Hang on.

Bihyeong took out a manual and began to read over it. After a long silence, he spoke.

......At this point, I don't even know who's the real goblin here.

He stared vacantly into the air, then shook his head and continued.

Fine. There's no problem with you using the shop. But due to regulations, the Goblin Shop can be only opened when the channel is online. You okay with that?

"That's fine."

[Channel #BI-7623 is online.]
[Constellations are entering.]

An electric flash, and a translucent screen appeared before my eyes.

[Welcome to the Goblin Shop.]

The Goblin Shop.

This was the "cash shop" of this messed-up world.

* * *

In the scenarios of *TWSA*, coins have two important uses.

One is to increase overall stats such as stamina or strength. The other is to serve as the common currency for shops like the one I was looking at now.

[Limited time offer! The Starter Pack is only 2,500 coins!]
[Special Sale! Grow faster than anyone with the 300% Growth Package!]
[Did you accidentally pick a crappy incarnation? Don't worry! A Random Attribute Box will randomly change your incarnation's attributes!]

A dizzying array of various packages and other items. All the ads were aimed at constellations looking to power up their incarnations. It made sense. The Goblin Shop was made for constellations to begin with.

I closed the pop-up ads one by one and organized my thoughts.

Compared to the legitimate calamities appearing after the fifth scenario, a sea commander was nothing. But in the early scenarios when the incarnations were still weak, it was almost an insurmountable force of nature.

It was crucial that I purchase a very specific set of items from the Goblin Shop, if I was to stand a chance of defeating the angler dragon. *Let's see...*

After flipping through the catalog for a while, I looked over at Bihyeong.

"Hey, is this all that's available for purchase? There should be a search function."

Oh, that's..... Damn it. Hang on. Dear constellations! Please calm down. Listen to me.

From the moment the channel had reopened, Bihyeong had been begging and pleading with his viewers, cartoonish beads of sweat dripping down his head.

It was just a server error! I didn't cut off the stream on purpose. I swear!

Currently, there were twenty-something stars shining above Bihyeong's head. Judging by the number that had come back, there were quite a lot of constellations watching me. Of course, not everyone was favorable toward me.

[A small number of constellations suspect foul play in this channel.]
[A small number of constellations are raising allegations that you are getting special treatment.]

I'd expected this to happen. Not only had a hidden scenario started while the channel was offline, but the Goblin Shop had been opened.

What? Special treatment? Please, I'm a goblin. I'd be disintegrated the moment I tried anything like that. C'mon, you know how strict the storyteller's oath is!

"Hey, a little help here?"

......The search button is in the bottom right corner.

"Thanks."

I left Bihyeong to struggle on his own and pressed the magnifying glass button hidden at the bottom of the package window.

[The item search function has been activated.]
[You are limited to five searches per day. You must pay 100 coins per additional search.]

Humans or goblins, exploitative business practices are the same everywhere.

The total number of searches I could do was five. It would only take two to find everything I needed, and I'd have three searches left.

[Constellation *Secretive Plotter* is curious about your plan.]

Of course you are. Watch closely.

[Constellation *Abyssal Black Flame Dragon* regards everything you do with annoyance.]

Don't like it? Then don't watch.
"Search 'Ancient Dragon.'"

[There are three results.]

Soon, a small pop-up window appeared.

* * *

The Heart of the Ancient Dragon - Stock: ?
The Bone of the Ancient Dragon - Stock: 1
The Horn of the Ancient Dragon - Stock: 1

* * *

I selected the Heart of the Ancient Dragon.

* * *

<Item Information>
Name: The Heart of the Ancient Dragon
Grade: SSS
Description: A heart imbued with the mana of the Ancient Dragon Ignitus. Contains near-limitless mana. Upon successful transplant, grants the "Hellfire" attribute.

Price: 1,500,000C
Stock: Just sold out.

* * *

As I thought, it was sold out. Bihyeong paused his efforts to placate the constellations and stared incredulously.

You crazy— How the hell do you know about the Ancient Dragon?

"I just typed something that seemed cool."

...Sounds like a lie.

I shrugged. According to *TWSA*, the owner of this heart was in Italy right now. *Lucky bastard. He has a filthy-rich sponsor who buys him high-level items like this.*

I searched for a few more items.

[Displaying search results.]

* * *

Arch Demon's Eyeball - Stock: 0
White Star Weapon Aura - Stock: 1

* * *

I couldn't believe the Arch Demon's Eyeball was sold out as well... Constellations sure are quick. Well, not that I could've afforded the one-million-coin price tag anyway. *Must be nice having a sponsor.* The incarnation who'd received the Arch Demon's Eyeball would have it on easy mode through the early scenarios and shoot ahead of everyone else.

What are you, really? Are you using some kinda cheat code? How do you know about the stuff that can only be viewed via the search function?

Out of the three items I'd searched for, the only one in stock was White Star Weapon Aura.

What, you're not gonna buy it?

"I can't right now. I'm just browsing."

Tch, then why did you make me open the shop?

"I'll buy something else, so bring up the items I call out."

Soon, a list appeared in front of me.

* * *

Hammer Seahorse's Mucus - Stock: 124
Stone Hog's Thorn - Stock: 17

* * *

I carefully checked the list against my memory. The hammer seahorse, an aquatic species that is a common prey of angler dragons, and the stone hog, which is a natural enemy of aquatic species… *I'm sure of it. This is the most efficient combination for dealing with an angler dragon.*

"Four bags of mucus and four thorns. Eight hundred coins should be enough, right?"

Yes, but...what're you gonna do with that junk?

"You don't need to know."

......I'm not trying to interfere, but how about purchasing something else? Like Moon Shadow Sword Technique. It's normally eight thousand coins, but I'll sell it to you now for only four thousand. It'll help you clear the scenario.

"Thanks, but I'll just take these."

Bihyeong seemed disappointed but sold me the items I asked for.

[You've spent 800 coins.]

Something like a cloud of shimmering dust began to coalesce in the darkness, until it turned into four long thorns and four pouches filled with mucus.

Well, it's too late to change your mind. No refunds. You know that, right?

"I know."

I nodded curtly and went to work. I took off my jacket and tied it into a loop, where I stuck the thorns. As for the pouches, I tied them around my waist.

A Stone Hog's Thorn is blunt on one side, but tapers into a sharp spike on the other side. It's about a meter long. Perfect for piercing something.

Hmm...... All right, then. I should get going. I can't stick around 'cause something interesting is happening outside, too.

"You do that."

Ha-ha. Good luck. May the blessing of the stories be with you.

Once the glowing goblin had disappeared, darkness fell once again. I could've used the flashlight on my phone, but I needed to save the battery as much as possible. Thankfully, the thorns emitted a bluish glow. It was quite dim, but I'd have to rely on that light source for a while.

I pulled one of the thorns from my waist and swung it a few times. Maybe it was because I didn't have any technical skills like "Weapon Proficiency" or "Man-at-Arms," but the thorn felt unwieldy in my hands.

[A small number of constellations are bored.]

It was about time for the more impatient constellations to leave the channel. Although I couldn't see from here, Bihyeong must've been feeling quite anxious, too.

Another hour passed.

Right, left, up, and down.

It still didn't feel quite right, but I could now wield the thorn without issue. It had a rough surface, so there was no danger of it slipping out of my grip, either.

Time to get started.

I stabbed the angler dragon's stomach lining with a reasonable amount of force.

Boing!

The thorn bounced right off as if it had hit a hard rubber wall. The angler dragon's stomach lining was too tough to pierce with my strength stat. Even if I used a skill, the result would be the same.

It was at that moment small holes near the top of the stomach opened all at once. With a loud gurgle, a torrent of revolting liquid gushed out of them.

"Kraaagh!"

A demonic being that was floating among the debris began to scream. The angler dragon had begun digesting. Its stomach acid quickly mixed with the river water and began to dissolve the chunks of concrete and other bits of debris, including the one I was standing on.

Fwoooosh!

...Time was running out. I had to proceed with my plan.

I jumped with all my strength off the floating panel and grabbed onto a bump on the stomach wall. Then I did my best imitation of a rock climber and slowly made my way up. Right above me, one of the open glands was gushing digestive acid. I held a thorn in my mouth and opened one of the bags at my waist.

Hammer Seahorse's Mucus.

I scooped out a bit of the weird-smelling black liquid and rubbed it all over the thorn. Like putting on shaving cream before a close shave, I thoroughly covered every bit of the thorn with the mucus. Just as shaving cream protects your face from the razor, this mucus would protect the thorn from the digestive acid.

Here goes nothing.

I pointed the thorn at a stomach acid gland. The angle was precise, and I used all the strength I had.

Kshk!

A bit of the corrosive fluid sprayed onto my arm and melted through the skin. But despite the horrific pain, I didn't stop. One mistake now, and it was game over.

[Exclusive skill "The Fourth Wall" partially alleviates the pain.]

Fwooosh. Slosh. Drip. Driiip...

At last, the thorn was wedged tightly into the gland.

"That's one down."

I paused briefly to catch my breath, then took out another thorn. Once again, I covered it with the Hammer Seahorse's Mucus and rammed it into another gland.

[A small number of constellations are impressed by your composure.]
[They have donated 200 coins.]

Rinse and repeat. I blocked three glands in the same way. There were a few smaller ones left, but not much stomach acid came out of those tiny openings. I controlled my breathing as I untied my jacket and wrapped it around the tip of a thorn that was lodged into the stomach wall.

I now had one thorn and two bags of mucus left. I smeared the mucus all over my body and clothes, and drank the rest.

"Ugh."

It left behind a salty and fishy aftertaste, but it was better than dying. This was nothing compared to the calamity I'd have to endure in the future.

At the five-minute mark, the angler dragon's stomach began to convulse violently.

Kraaaaaah—!

* * *

The gargantuan beast roared in pain. The veins lining the stomach wall were reddening. It was going as planned. Nestled among the veins, the thorns that were rammed into the glands began their metabolic activity. I recalled this information from *TWSA*.

A Stone Hog's Thorn reacts to the bodily fluids of aquatic species.

Crack. Craaaack.

The thorns were immune to the corrosive effect of the digestive juice, thanks to their coat of mucus. They began to absorb the angler dragon's bodily fluid and spread their roots into the monster's body. The Stone Hog's Thorns wouldn't stop growing until the angler dragon was completely dead.

Kraaaah—!

I looked down at the swirling pool of deadly liquid below me and gripped the thorn tightly. I'd done everything I could. The rest was a matter of willpower.

Either I die, or this monster dies.

There will only be one survivor.

4

I couldn't tell how much time had passed. I had trouble breathing, and muscles all over my body had grown stiff or seized up entirely.

> [A small number of constellations are impressed by your will to survive!]
> [They have donated 100 coins.]

But I held on. I endured because I believed I could endure. I looked to the faint glow of the thorns in the darkness to assure myself that I was still alive. And I felt the monster's stomach wall as it slowly grew cold to assure myself that it was dying.

> [Constellation *Demonic Judge of Fire* is amazed by your persistence.]
> [They have donated 100 coins.]

When I was hungry, I moved my mouth near the thorn and lapped up the fluid that seeped out of it. The concentrate contained the angler dragon's life essence that was being sucked out by the thorn. The reason I'd drank the Hammer Seahorse's Mucus previously was so that I could safely consume this concentrate.

[You have absorbed the angler dragon's power. Your stamina has increased slightly.]

I hadn't consumed enough of it to gain stat points yet, but by the time I made it out of here, I should have gained about two points of stamina. It was one of a few tricks to boost your stamina early on without spending coins.

...This isn't a dream, is it?

Vague thoughts drifted through my consciousness like passages of a novel.

Can I really do this?
I'm just an ordinary reader.
Not the main character.

It felt like I'd wake up screaming on my bed at any moment, but no matter how many times I closed and opened my eyes, no such miracle happened.

......I wonder if mother is okay.
I'm sure she is. It's mother *I'm talking about.*

Every time digestive acid drained from the bottom of the stomach, I drifted off to sleep. And every time cold river water poured in from the gullet, I jolted awake.

Then, at last, the angler dragon's digestive cycle stopped. Its stomach wall, pressed against my back, rapidly lost its warmth, and the supple texture of its viscera grew rigid.

The angler dragon was dead.

* * *

......That's incredible.

A bright electric current pierced the darkness. The blurry shape of Bihyeong was floating in midair.

Who knew a Stone Hog's Thorn could be used like that? I had no idea. Did you?

Bihyeong spoke as he eyed the Stone Hog's Thorn glowing faintly in the dark.

Stone hogs live near the shore and eat small aquatic species. They pierce their prey's body with these thorns to desiccate them. To think he'd jam them into the stomach acid gland...

Bihyeong's glowing eyes weren't looking at me. Naturally, his explanation wasn't meant for me, either.

[A very small number of constellations smile knowingly.]
[They have donated 100 coins.]
[A small number of constellations finally understand what you were doing.]
[Constellations complain that you should talk to yourself while doing these things so they can understand what's going on.]

I ignored the constellations' messages and drank the last of the concentrate.

[You have absorbed the angler dragon's power.]
[Your stamina has increased!]
[Stamina Lv.11 -> Stamina Lv.12]

With that, I'd accomplished my goals. Bihyeong floated down next to me and continued with his commentary, touching my arm to bring attention to the blackened skin.

And this...... Even I didn't know Hammer Seahorse's Mucus had this kind of effect...

My skin should've been melted off by the angler dragon's stomach acid. I picked up where Bihyeong had trailed off.

"Hammer Seahorse's Mucus protects against digestive fluid. They evolved this way because they're often preyed upon by angler dragons."

[A small number of constellations are impressed by your knowledge.]

Bihyeong shot me a look of betrayal.

Excuse me, explaining is my job...

"Well, it sounded like you didn't know what you were talking about. Anyway, are you done with your nature documentary?"

......Yes.

"Then give me my reward."

You snarky little—!

As Bihyeong grumbled, the reward messages began to appear.

[The hidden scenario has ended.]
[You have received 9,000 coins as a reward.]
[You have become the first person to successfully hunt a level-7 aquatic species.]
[You have received 1,000 coins as a reward for this achievement.]

Nine thousand coins, plus an extra thousand. Not bad at all.

[Coins Owned: 14,800C]

Including the five hundred I'd received as donations during my unexpected stint as an extreme survival streamer, my total earnings amounted to ten thousand five hundred coins. This was well above my goal.

Ha-ha, did you all enjoy that? We'll be right back with the next scenario after a quick commercial break!

With that, I heard the muted sound of a commercial. "Special package for a new scenario! Eight thousand eight hundred coins, limited time only!" and so on…… With the constellations' eyes no longer on us, Bihyeong floated down to me and spoke, sounding nothing but friendly.

Phew...... What a banger of a survival scenario. The constellations' reactions were incredible, too.

"How long has it been?"

Four days. Four nerve-racking days. You didn't even know how many days had passed?

"My phone battery was dead."

This had taken much longer than I'd planned. My original goal had been two days…… Still, it wasn't a bad record, considering Junghyeok Yu also took four days to do this on his fourth loop.

Anyway, I'd done it. A pleasant wave of satisfaction washed over me and boosted my confidence. I was a normal person with ordinary abilities. But that didn't mean I was limited to only achieving ordinary things.

"…How funny."

It was strange. A work of fiction that had been useless to me all my life had transformed this ordinary human into an extraordinary one.

Ooh, you're already speaking your thoughts out loud?

"……"

You're a natural, aren't you? Talking to yourself is a must for any incarnation looking to put on a good show. Of course, some constellations don't like it 'cause it seems too contrived, but—

"Whatever. Just open the Goblin Shop already."

Why? Is there something you want to buy?

"Buying and selling both."

Ugh, then I'll have to cut the commercials short. Dear constellations, let me check the audio real quick.

While Bihyeong was opening the shop, I surveyed the thorns in the angler dragon's stomach wall. As the stomach wall had dried up and hardened, cracks had formed around the thorns. The stomach lining had become brittle enough for me to break apart with my strength stat.

I dug deeper and deeper, picking at the crack with the last remaining thorn. Soon, I came upon an object shining with a brilliant blue light.

[Angler Dragon's Nucleus]

It was an aether core found in a level-7 or higher monster. A valuable item that can increase your magic power if processed and consumed. And since it was coming from a sea commander–level angler dragon, it was in pristine quality. I carefully cut the nucleus out of the flesh. Bihyeong looked at me incredulously.

"I'm selling it."

Seriously, you—

"But I'm not selling it to you. Put it up for auction."

It looked like Bihyeong had given up trying to ask questions and had decided to just accept what I was doing.

Haah... Whatever. So how much do you want to list it for?

"No coins. Exchange only."

Damn, how do you know all this stuff?

Bihyeong grumbled but put it up for auction as I'd asked. *He may be single-mindedly greedy, but he's pretty easy to work with.*

"Someone will want to buy it soon. Make sure it's traded for Broken Faith."

Broken Faith? Would anyone even have that...? Anyway, I registered the auction.

"Okay. And I want to buy......"

I looked at White Star Weapon Aura in the shop. As I'd thought, no one had bought it yet. Most of the constellations didn't know which items had good value. The Goblin Shop used every trick in the book to empty out the constellations' pockets, and a higher price tag didn't always mean higher quality.

Wait. Before that, can we talk first?

The volume of the commercials went up again after Bihyeong spoke.

[Constellations are complaining about the long commercial break.]

I saw that the same ads were being looped, and realized what Bihyeong was about to say.

"Is it about the contract?"

The commercial break was the only way to block out viewers without shutting off the channel. And what we were about to discuss was not something the constellations should hear.

Yeah. I was on the fence, but watching you clear this scenario convinced me. Well...let's give it a shot. It won't be easy, but I can bail you out here and there.

"That's against the storyteller's oath, isn't it?"

Oh, of course I can't blatantly help you. I was just saying. Anyway, you'll sign it, right?

"What are the terms?"

Read it for yourself.

Bihyeong had already prepared the contract. *Typical goblin.*

I began reading the contract that appeared in a holographic window.

* * *

<Stream Contract Agreement>
Incarnation Dokja Kim [Party A] will form an exclusive contract with Goblin Bihyeong [Party B], effective until all scenarios are completed or he dies.

* * *

"…I'm Party A?"

Ha-ha. Humans obsess over that stuff, right? Even though it's meaningless here. Anyway, keep reading.

* * *

2. Party A must not choose a sponsoring constellation until all scenarios are completed or he dies.

I'd expected this part.

3. Party A must only appear in the channel run by Party B.
4. Party A and Party B will share all profits coming from the stream contract. Ratio to be agreed upon.

…

10. Should Party A or Party B breach this contract, they will be disintegrated, in accordance with Star Stream regulations.

* * *

I carefully read to the last line. The contract was surprisingly well written. I'd fully expected the goblin to try to take advantage of me with all kinds of loopholes and hidden clauses, but it was actually quite fair and straightforward.

Well, except for one thing.

"There's an important part that's missing."

You mean signatures? You can just say you agree. A stream contract is a soul oath, so—

"I'm talking about the ratio."

O-oh. Ha-ha. Right.

Tch, acting like he forgot. That was the most important part. Bihyeong hesitated for a bit, then spoke up like he was doing me a great favor.

How about an even half-half? And I'll waive your channel usage fees. Oh, you know how to calculate the profit, right? We'll evenly split all the donations you receive. For example, if you receive a hundred coins, we each take fifty.

This was how stream contracts worked. A constellation would have their incarnation appear on a goblin's channel and would split the donations the incarnation received from other constellations. That was how profits were divided...under normal circumstances.

"You think I'm stupid? I'm not signing this."

What? But that's the industry standard...

"I'm an incarnation without a sponsor. In order to donate coins to someone like me, constellations have to pay an exorbitant commission to the goblin. You've been making bank from that, haven't you?"

Bihyeong's jaw fell open. I ignored his cartoonish expression and continued.

"Ten to zero. You'll be set with the commissions alone. I'm not giving you a single coin."

What? That's ridiculous... H-how about seven to three?

This was a big increase from his initial offer, but I wasn't compromising.

"Ten to zero."

You've gotta be kidding me! Ten to zero? That's bull—

"Never mind, then. I'll go to a different channel. I hear Gildal's channel is trending these days. So I should try there."

...Eight to two. I can't go lower than that.

"Ten to zero."

......

Bihyeong's face turned scary. He looked ready to make my head explode at any moment. But I knew he couldn't give up on this contract. *After all, I'm the last hope he's got.*

"The ads are almost over. Can't you see the constellations complaining?"

Finally, Bihyeong seemed to give up.

Damn it, fine. So do we have a deal?

Oh? He'd given in much more easily than I'd expected. The truth is, I was willing to settle for nine to one... Maybe this bastard was making even more money from commissions than I'd thought. *How annoying.*

"Oh, one more thing."

What? There's more?

"The signing bonus is not included. My five thousand coins. Cough it up."

Bihyeong stared at me blankly.

Seriously, you're...

I smiled. *You stupid goblin, I'll show you why humans care so much about being Party A. The things you can do with a contract if you're Party A...*

[The stream contract has been signed.]
[You have received 5,000 coins as a signing bonus.]

Soon after, the ads ended, and constellations returned to the channel. I patted the goblin's shoulder.

"Now then, shall I get out of here?"

This is where the real game starts.

EPISODE

04

Hypocrisy Can Be a Virtue

1

A meteor shower was falling across the night sky. Most people would have been awed by this spectacle, but not Junghyeok Yu.

[Is it starting?]

After all, the meteor shower was an omen that the third scenario was on the horizon. Seoul would perish as planned.

Junghyeok looked down from the night sky to the mouth of the Han River. The swarm of angler dragons had migrated downriver, so it was quite peaceful around Dongho Bridge.

[I guess it was too much for him.]

It had been three days since Dokja Kim had fallen into the river. A beginner who had just cleared the first scenario, hunting an angler dragon? That was probably too much to ask for.

[Well, even I would have a hard time doing that in three days.]

Still, if this Dokja Kim couldn't manage that, then he wasn't worth taking along. He'd just be a liability.

[He called himself a Prophet, but I guess he wasn't all that.]

* * *

Junghyeok closed his eyes in disappointment. He'd move forward on his own once again. No allies. It wasn't a big deal. He'd always been alone.

[This time, I'll change the future no matter what.]

Junghyeok turned around.

But perhaps he'd given up too soon.

"Wait…!"

Wh-what?

I blinked several times, but all I could see was a grayish-white ceiling. I was still inside the angler dragon's stomach. When I turned my head, Bihyeong was there, looking startled.

"…I had a dream."

Ooh, an ominous foreshadowing to get the constellations hooked? Classic. You really are a natural, aren't you?

That wasn't what I was doing, but I didn't care enough to correct him.

> [A small number of constellations wish you'd move to a new location already.]

I'd fallen asleep after using the Ellain Forest Essence I'd bought for five hundred coins. It was too dangerous to make a move while I was this exhausted.

Ellain Forest Essence put you to sleep for two hours, but quickly healed your wounds and fatigue. It had a hefty price tag, but it was worth every coin.

"…I really should get going now," I muttered to myself as I stretched. The dream I'd had was still vivid in my mind. Perhaps it hadn't been a dream.

Bzzzt.

There was an electric crackle, and Bihyeong disappeared without a word. I was sure he had work to do elsewhere.

I sighed in relief.

A stream contract with a goblin. It was a gamble I couldn't have attempted if I hadn't read about Bihyeong in *TWSA*. Looking back, I was surprised by how calm and collected I'd been throughout that tense situation. Even though I'd struggled to lock down even the smallest contracts in "real life."

[Exclusive skill "The Fourth Wall" has been activated.]

...Real life, huh? I clenched the thorn I held in my right hand. Did I really consider this to be reality?

[A small number of constellations want you to get moving already.]

Well, it wasn't the time to be worrying about this stuff. I gripped the thorn and swung hard at the stomach wall, breaking open the brittle dead tissue. Water gushed in, and I jumped into the Han River.

"Pwah!"

Luckily, there were no other angler dragons around. Small aquatic species approached curiously, but they didn't seem hostile. Not all monsters attacked humans.

...Is Dongho Bridge that way?

I used a chunk of the dead angler dragon as a flotation device and kicked awkwardly at the water. The cold water stung my skin, but I ignored it. After about thirty minutes of swimming, I finally reached the shore.

[A small number of constellations tense up.]

This kind of message usually meant something dangerous was about to happen.

[Constellation *Abyssal Black Flame Dragon* grins ominously.]

Too bad for the constellations who disliked me, but it wouldn't go the way they wanted. I already knew exactly what hazards lay ahead.

[You have entered the zone of the second scenario.]
[This scenario zone is heavily polluted.]
[Hold your breath and quickly seek shelter in an underground area.]

That was how the message explained it, but from the very moment the scenario started, you weren't supposed to be aboveground. What was happening to my skin was proof of that.

[You have been exposed to a poisonous fog.]

My skin was turning black as soon as it came in contact with the purple fog.

Groar!

As I tracked the source of the purple fog, I spotted a monster which was letting out a horrendous roar.

A towering behemoth over thirty meters tall.

This fog was the flatulence of a level-7 monster, a plague rhinoceros. It snorted as it faced another monster across the fog. Based on its silhouette, the other monster appeared to be a monarch species insect.

Kreee...

It wasn't just humans who were struggling to survive in the new world. Monsters fought for territory as well.

I tried my best to hold my breath as I moved. They were level-7 monsters like the sea commander, but I wouldn't be able to handle them now. I'd been able to kill the sea commander because I was ready.

[You are using Ellain Monkey's Lung.]

An item that can neutralize poison for twenty minutes. I'd purchased it from Bihyeong in preparation for this.

[A small number of constellations are impressed by your readiness!]

Oksu Station was destroyed, since it was aboveground. The closest underground station was Geumho. The others should've already moved there.

I quickly made my way through the streets, avoiding small monsters feasting on dead bodies. I only had twenty minutes to gather the necessary supplies and reach my destination.

The first thing I needed was clothes. Mine had been damaged by the angler dragon's stomach acid. There were plenty of clothes around, but I didn't feel good about taking them.

...I had no choice, though. I took some clothes off the dead bodies that were strewn about. Next, I made a beeline to a convenience store. I hurriedly scooped some small and compact food items into a few plastic bags. Once underground, these would serve as great bargaining chips.

I'd collected about three or four bags of food when I noticed that the monkey's lung I was holding in my mouth was starting to turn black. I was running out of time. Just then, I heard a voice.

"H-help…please help me…"

…Someone's still alive out here? I turned my head and saw a young woman cowering in a corner. Her arms and shoulders were bruised as if she had been fighting, and her ripped shirt had bloodstains. Luckily, her wounds weren't deep, but the effects of the poison were evident on her skin.

The face mask she was wearing was slowing down the effect of the poison, but she would be dead soon if I left her here.

"Are you okay? Can you get up?"

"Ughh…"

I wanted to check if there was a minor character like her in *TWSA*, but there was no time. I carried her on my back and ran straight toward Geumho Station.

I made my way down a side street until I came upon a large road. Geumho Station was only a hundred meters straight ahead from here. Taking a deep breath, I dashed down the road at full speed. I could see Exit 3 in the distance.

…Closed. What about the other side?

Every exit had the shutters down. It must have been standard protocol for a state of emergency. I could've broken through with the Stone Hog's Thorn, but that might endanger the people inside.

"Four… Exit 4…"

Unexpectedly, the woman on my back helped me. As I ran toward Exit 4, I could hear the shutters being lowered. I stuck the thorn into the gap before it could fully close. Someone yelled.

"Wh-what the hell?!"

"Open the door."

"No! You can't come in! Go away!"

"I have an injured person with me."

"It's already full in here. We don't need any more people!"

It's full? They won't take any more people? Strange. Did this happen in the novel?

"I don't care."

I used the thorn as a lever to lift up the shutter. I'd used coins to get my strength stat up to level 10, so I had the strength of five or six adult men.

"Aaaack!"

The people who'd been trying to lower the shutter were thrown off their feet.

"R-run!"

Those men got scared and disappeared into the darkness underground. Safely inside, I closed the shutter behind me and put the woman down.

[You have entered a safe zone.]

The poisonous fog didn't go underground. That may not be how gases behave, but not everything in a scenario required a scientific explanation.

"Put this in your mouth."

I took the mask off the woman's face and put the monkey's lung I'd been using in her mouth. *It won't heal her completely, but it'll neutralize some of the poison.*

"Ngh…"

She let out a faint moan.

An abandoned woman. I was curious about her. Chances are, she was supposed to have died back there. But as I was about to activate "Character Profile," I heard a voice.

"Over there! That's him!"

From the darkness, flashlights were approaching. Once I squinted, I could make out a group of men armed with iron pipes and such.

[Constellation *Prisoner of the Golden Headband* frowns at the appearance of the unwelcome guests.]

A large man in the middle was the first to speak. Judging by his physique, he was probably no stranger to fighting.

"Who the hell are you?"

For some reason, I couldn't answer. *How do I respond in a situation like this?* I thought about it for a moment, then put on my best Junghyeok Yu impression.

"Dokja Kim."

"...Dokja Kim? That's your name?"

"Yes."

"I didn't ask for your damn name! Who the hell are you?"

It was even harder to answer that question.

"Wh-what? That woman..."

One of the men shined his flashlight on the woman beside me.

"Huh? Isn't she from the minor group? I thought she came back with the rest of you guys."

"Uh, about that..."

The man flicked his flashlight around the woman's waist in a vulgar manner. The large man chuckled knowingly.

"Ah-ha. I see, you filthy dogs. Ya didn't even ask me for permission first...?"

"Heh...heh-heh. Apologies, sir."

"I-I know you should get first dibs, Cheolsu... Heh-heh. We were going to, but..."

Cheolsu? Cheolsu... Had there been a character by that name? Well, I didn't remember him, so he must have been a small fry despite how he looked.

"Hand over the woman and— Huh? What's that?"

The flashlight's beam was now on the convenience store bags. This was taking a dangerous turn.

"Leave those, too, and get outta here. Then maybe I won't kill you."
Dangerous for them, not me.

[Constellation ***Prisoner of the Golden Headband*** is annoyed by the appearance of small fries.]
[Constellation ***Demonic Judge of Fire*** is furious about the breach of justice.]
[A bounty scenario has been started at the request of constellations.]

* * *

<Bounty Scenario — Get Rid of the Nuisance>
Category: Sub
Difficulty: F
Mission: Constellations are furious at the petty villains dragging down the pacing of the story. Take care of them within the time limit.
Time Limit: 5 minutes
Reward: ???
Penalty for Failure: ???

* * *

I'd thought this might happen. *Poor bastards.*
I straightened up, holding the thorn in my hand.
There aren't any underage constellations watching this, right? I hope not. Things are about to get graphic.

2

Sometimes I wonder.

Why do so many post-apocalyptic stories feature cliché villains?

Do the authors just assume there'll be wanton rape and robbery because they're too lazy to write complex villains? If the apocalypse actually happened, wouldn't people behave in a rational manner?

"He's not leaving? Kill him!"

The answer to that question was in front of my eyes. The group of thugs warily slinking toward me. And the man standing in the back watching it all, as though taking in beautiful scenery.

> [Constellation *Demonic Judge of Fire* is looking forward to righteous judgment.]

This reminded me—human imagination is boring and predictable, but actual humans are even more boring and predictable. One of the men awkwardly swung his iron pipe. It didn't seem like it was meant to be a killing blow. I doubt it would've hurt even if the hit had connected.

"Buzz off, or I'll kill you for real! Scram!"

Four men surrounded me. One of them was shaking a bit, but they seemed more confident than before. It was probably because they outnumbered me.

"Why are you just standing there?!"

Finally, a man yelled and charged at me. He was so full of openings that I almost felt bad. I swung my thorn.

"Gaaah! My leg! My leg!"

He collapsed to the ground, clutching the gaping wound on his thigh.

"That crazy bastard!"

"Everyone, attack at the same time!"

They came at me all at once, but I wasn't afraid. Their strength stats were around five. I just stood there as they hit me, and stabbed with my thorn. One by one, they dropped to the ground, screaming in pain while clutching their thighs. But I didn't kill them. The mission for the bounty scenario had only said to "take care of" them.

[Constellations of the absolute good alignment nod in approval of your decision.]
[A small number of constellations scoff at your sense of morality.]
[They have donated 100 coins.]

Brutal murder might get you the constellations' attention, but only for a moment. Dialing up the shock value too much at once is not smart in the long run.

[Three minutes remain until the end of the sub scenario.]

I'd used up two minutes so far. Efficient management of time was crucial for scenarios with time limits.

"Wh-what is this bastard? Why isn't he dead already?"

Finally, the leader who'd been watching from the back stepped forward.

"Hmm, he's tougher than he looks. Y'all fall back. I'll deal with him."

"Cheolsu, sir! That bastard must have a sponsoring constellation!"
"Good. He must have plenty of coins, then."
His brass knuckles gleamed a slick black. They weren't an ordinary weapon. Had he gotten them from his sponsoring constellation?
Cheolsu cracked his knuckles.

[Character *Cheolsu Bang* has activated the stigma "Threaten."]
["Threaten" failed due to a large gap between his stats and yours.]

"Oh? You've got balls. Most idiots would be pissing their pants by now."

The man was throwing a punch before he'd even finished his sentence. A precise strike aimed at my chin. He grinned when I stepped back to dodge the attack.

"Not bad. You do martial arts or something?"

Anyone with an agility stat over ten could do this, even without a skill. After buying the items I needed, I'd invested most of my remaining coins on my stats, bringing the total of my stamina, strength, and agility up to thirty-three.

Let's see what this guy's stats are.

[Exclusive skill "Character Profile" has been activated.]

* * *

<Character Profile>
Name: Cheolsu Bang
Age: 34
Sponsoring Constellation: Monarch of the Small Fries
Exclusive Attribute: Assault Captain [Common]

Exclusive Skills: [Dogfight Lv.2], [Bluff Lv.2]
Stigma: [Threaten Lv.1]
Total Stats: [Stamina Lv.6], [Strength Lv.7], [Agility Lv.7], [Magic Power Lv.2]
Summary: A small-time crook who got lucky and obtained a sponsoring constellation. He has a tendency to overestimate his abilities.

* * *

Ah...I see. I remember now.

"Cheolsu Bang of the Cheoldu Gang."

"Huh? You know who I am?"

"Maybe."

He'd only appeared briefly near the beginning of the story, so I could only recall vaguely, but I did remember a character named Cheolsu Bang. He was the dumbest character among the groups at Geumho Station. According to the novel, he should've been killed by Junghyeok Yu, so why was he still alive?

"Ah, I get it now. You're on 'this side,' too. Killed a bunch of people, haven't you? I can tell you and I are of the same breed."

[Character *Cheolsu Bang* has activated the skill "Bluff."]

"Bluff." A skill commonly possessed by thugs like him. *It's a good debuff against an opponent with a weak mind, but that's not the case here.*

["The Fourth Wall" has blocked character *Cheolsu Bang*'s attempt to bluff.]
[Character *Cheolsu Bang*'s confidence has greatly decreased.]

"Are you ignoring me? That's it. I'll kill you."

Cheolsu posed Greco-Roman wrestler style, like he was about to charge me. But that was a bluff, too. I knew he didn't have any wrestling skills.

"Hurry up before I die of boredom."

"What did you say?! You little—!"

Cheolsu Bang's main skill was level-2 Dogfight.

As long as the fight didn't turn into a messy brawl, he was laughably weak.

"Die!"

Due the difference in our agility stats, he couldn't land a hit on me. I looked at him with pity.

Not every constellation had the desire to make their incarnation the main character of the scenarios. Unfortunately for Cheolsu, Monarch of the Small Fries was notorious for not caring about their incarnations. They'd just find some idiot they could toy with for a bit, and get a kick out of watching the poor fool get beaten up by another incarnation. A real masochist. That was Monarch of the Small Fries.

[Constellation *Monarch of the Small Fries* is entertained.]
[Constellation *Monarch of the Small Fries* has donated 100 coins.]

Just look at that sick bastard, rooting for the enemy who's pummeling their incarnation.

I'd been planning to finish Cheolsu off since there was a time limit, but this changed things.

[Two minutes remain until the end of the sub scenario.]

Time to milk every last second.

"You little rat!"

Cheolsu even talked the way Monarch of the Small Fries loved. *Poor guy.*

Pow!

"Ha-ha. I hit him!"

By sheer luck, he'd landed a hit, but it didn't hurt at all. I just felt a slight sting.

"Wait— How?"

What do you mean, "how"? My stamina stat was twelve. And that guy's strength stat was only seven. Having a different first digit in total stats values results in a huge gap in combat power.

"It's my turn, right?" I said.

Cheolsu looked stunned. I gently patted his face a few times before slapping him with all my strength. A couple of his teeth flew out of his mouth, and he rolled to the ground with a scream.

Without missing a beat, I pierced his arm with my thorn.

"Aaargh!"

I pinned one of his arms to the wall with the thorn and beat him relentlessly. His back, thighs, and waist. I only hit the parts that would cause the most pain without knocking him unconscious.

[Constellation *Monarch of the Small Fries* is delighted.]
[Constellation *Monarch of the Small Fries* has requested to extend the sub scenario time.]
[The sub scenario has been extended for one more minute.]

The spots I was hitting mirrored where the woman had been wounded.

"Gaah! Argh! Gyaaaah!"

Flesh tore and blood spurted. Broken teeth clattered to the ground. Cheolsu's joints were bent at all the wrong angles. Still, I continued to kick him.

"S-stop! Let him go!"

His men sounded panicked. I looked at each of them, then at the woman lying on the ground.

Humans are weak. So how were these weaklings capable of such cruelty just because the world had ended? They killed, raped, and robbed other humans.

Because of human nature?

In the face of a greater violence, Cheolsu's eyes were filled with fear. I became curious.

"Why did you do it?"

The question came out of nowhere, so I wasn't expecting an answer. But as I was about to kick him again, he glared at me.

"Shit…shit! Just kill me already, you bastard."

Looking at his eyes, I realized he'd answered my question in his own way. There was no attachment to life in his eyes. *I see.* It wasn't instinct that drove him.

Cheolsu's voice faded as he mumbled.

"Screw this world, this shitty hellhole…"

This man had been in despair long before the world had ended. *Just like me.*

[Ten seconds remain until the end of the sub scenario.]

Without further delay, I kicked him hard in the neck.

Cheolsu let out a weak groan, then finally passed out.

[You have fulfilled the conditions of the sub scenario.]
[You have obtained 300 coins.]

I'm sure this was enough to please that sick bastard.

[Constellation *Monarch of the Small Fries* is satisfied and has donated 100 coins as a bonus.]

The rest of the men were crawling over one by one.

"H-how cruel..."

They checked on Cheolsu's ruined body, then gazed up at me without a word. They looked like animals at the slaughterhouse. I put the woman on my back and grabbed the convenience store bags.

The old world was no more, and I had to live my new life.

"Take me to where the groups are."

* * *

Originally, Geumho Station was supposed to develop into a central hub after being cleaned up and reorganized by Junghyeok Yu.

In his first loop, Junghyeok cleared the second scenario with the group at Geumho, so the people here had ended up being key supporting characters. But that was just the first loop. Third-loop Junghyeok was a different beast altogether.

In the third loop, Junghyeok is a monster who takes everything for himself.

"...Still, I thought he'd do some basic cleanup before moving on."

"Pardon?"

The man who was guiding me asked nervously.

"Just talking to myself. It's a habit."

[Constellation *Secretive Plotter* is pleased that you talk to yourself.]

"Oh, okay... It's this way."

Members of the Cheoldu Gang who were leaning on each other to walk came to a stop. I made my way down to the darkened platform. Some sections still had electricity. As soon as we went down the stairs, people began to murmur.

"It's the Cheoldu Gang! They're hurt!"

Some people ran to help Cheolsu and his men. They were more organized than I'd expected and moved in a surprisingly orderly manner. Then I saw some familiar faces running toward me.

"My gosh, Dokja! It's Dokja!"

Luckily, they seemed fine.

"Sangah."

"Thank goodness, I'm so glad!"

Sangah stood in front of me, looking like she didn't know what to do with herself. I awkwardly extended a hand for a handshake. There were small cuts and scrapes all over her hand. She must've been through a lot these past four days.

Fwump—I felt someone hug my legs.

Gilyeong Lee. I patted the boy's head.

"You doing all right?"

Gilyeong nodded. He must not have been eating properly, judging by his sunken cheeks. I took out a candy bar and put it in his hand.

"You're alive, Dokja. Phew..."

The last person to welcome me was Hyeonseong Lee. His upper body looked even more muscular than I remembered. He'd likely been fighting to protect the other two.

"I'm so sorry we had to leave you behind..."

"It's okay. You had no choice."

"Whew, good thing Mr. Junghyeok Yu was right."

...Junghyeok Yu? Why was that name coming up now? Hyeonseong looked at me and continued.

"Well, he said you were probably still alive..."

"Where is he now?"

"Um, he's not here."

Not here?

"He left this station yesterday, so..."

Even before Hyeonseong had finished, I was able to deduce a few things.

I see. I get it now. What an impatient guy.

"By the way, it looks like someone else is missing."

"Oh, you mean Mr. Han? He's—"

Sangah was interrupted by a group of men rushing in. But that was a good thing.

"Get out of the way!"

Because I could see at a glance what had happened without Sangah having to explain. Several men, each brandishing a hammer or a pipe, surrounded me. I spotted a familiar face at the center of the group.

"You...!"

Myeongoh, who had abandoned me on the Bridge of Even Numbers, looked at me as if I were a ghost. How very like him to join that group.

"Kick him out. He's bad news! He shouldn't be here!"

Terrified that I was here to get revenge, Myeongoh yelled hysterically. But the other men only exchanged uneasy glances.

Something was off. Myeongoh Han wasn't their boss?

"Ha-ha, Mr. Han. Come on, now. We survivors should get along, no?"

"Well, th-the thing is..."

"Ah, you must be the newest addition to our group."

The thugs stepped aside to make way as a slim man walked up from the back of the crowd. One look at his eyes, and I could tell. This guy had a sponsoring constellation.

"Nice to meet you. May I ask your name?"

"I'm Dokja Kim."

"Dokja Kim. I see. I'm Inho Cheon."

Inho Cheon? That sounds familiar... I gripped the thorn tightly. The Cheoldu Gang must have been his lackeys. Had he come to get revenge on me for what I'd done to them?

"I heard everything from the others. You fought the monsters and saved our group members, right?"

...Eh?

"Everyone, please, gather around. We have a brave new team member."

With that, people began to approach one by one.

I knew it. Myeongoh Han didn't have the charisma to lead a group of this size. This man was the true leader of Geumho Station.

"Whoa! It's food!"

The people were hungry, and their eyes were on the plastic bags in my hand. Inho spoke as if he'd been waiting for this.

"He says he brought food for us. How generous of him, right?"

There were gasps of relief, and I became the center of attention. A mother holding her child, an old man with an injured leg...everyone was staring at me with desperation in their eyes.

Inho Cheon... I think I remember him now. That's right, this bastard was in Geumho.

[Constellation *Secretive Plotter* is agitated.]

In a fallen world, the truly dangerous people aren't the ones who have gone mad from despair, like Cheolsu Bang. It's the ones who use other people's despair to seize power. *Like this one.*

"Welcome to Geumho Station, Mr. Dokja Kim."

Inho Cheon was extending his hand with a friendly smile. I smiled back at him and shook his hand.

I bet he has no idea...that his fate has been sealed just now.

3

Despite everything Inho Cheon had done, the constellations didn't request a bounty scenario.

In other words, this wasn't the right time to take care of him.

For the next several hours, I focused on figuring out the current situation at Geumho Station. Hyeonseong was my primary source of information.

"Currently, there are eighty-six people here. Oh, I guess it's eighty-seven now, including you."

"That's fewer than I thought."

"Yes. Only people who were near the station or on the train made it when the scenario started. No one talks about it, but every single person here got through the first scenario..."

He didn't say the rest, but I knew. I could see it in the people's eyes. They had taken the lives of others to survive. Everyone here was a murderer.

"Geumho Station is currently divided into two groups. Well, I suppose it's more like one group and the rest."

Hyeonseong cast a gloomy look at the people nearby. Men armed with steel pipes. It was obvious who was in the main group.

"Trust me! The chairman will spare no expense until we're rescued."

Manager Myeongoh Han, Hankyeong Corporation's youngest son.

"Mr. Han is right, everyone. Don't lose hope. We can make it out of here."

And the man behind Myeongoh who held the true power, Inho Cheon. Their faction was the major group.

"I'm bored, Mom... Can I play a game on the phone?"

"Just wait a little longer. The rescue team will be here soon."

"I'm telling you. The government will do something. Korea couldn't have fallen that easily."

The rest of the people under the major group's protection, trying to get by however they could, was the minor group.

Looking at their listless faces, it was hard to believe they'd killed other people just a few days ago. Gather a hundred murderers, and they'll divide themselves into the strong and the weak. Perhaps these people didn't consider themselves murderers. Maybe they told themselves they had no choice.

Hyeonseong continued, watching the major group incite the others.

"The major group is in charge of distributing food. They already took everything from the convenience store and restaurants located inside this station... Supplies are running low."

"I see."

"So they've been assigning people to go out and look for more. Like Huiwon, who was traveling with us."

"Huiwon? You mean..."

"Oh, that's the name of the one you rescued."

I looked at the woman lying on a bench. Thanks to the monkey's lung, her face looked better than it had this morning.

"Is she the only one who was left behind?"

"No. Actually, there were a few more who went aboveground this morning, but no one from the minor group made it back."

"They didn't come back?"

"No."

Hyconseong looked distressed again. I was starting to get an idea of how things worked around here. I grabbed Hyeonseong's shoulder. As soon as I touched him, I knew why he was called Steel Blade. His strength stat was probably over ten.

"Wh-what's wrong?"

"Hyeonseong, why didn't you join the major group? I'm sure they tried to get you on their side."

"Oh, that..."

Hyeonseong scratched his cheek as if embarrassed.

"I'm not sure how to explain it, but I just felt that I shouldn't. I don't know much about higher ethics or morals...but I had a feeling that the major group wasn't in the right."

Not in the right...

It was a simple yet honest answer.

How very like him.

"Never forget the way you feel right now."

That way, I can always count on you.

Grumble.

I heard a cute sound and noticed that Gilyeong and Sangah were watching me from behind. They so resembled a pair of baby birds waiting for their mother that I couldn't help but crack a smile.

"Oh, isn't it almost dinnertime? You must be hungry. Take one each."

I gave them some food from the convenience store.

"Really? You don't mind?"

"It's free this time, but I'll start charging you next time."

"Sorry? How much...?"

"You all have coins, right? I'll start charging you ten coins per item."

"I see..."

Sangah and Hyeonseong looked taken aback. They clearly hadn't been expecting me to do that.

"Of course you should charge for them. Here, I'll start paying now. I don't want a free lunch."

Surprisingly, the voice came from Huiwon Jeong, who had been lying on the bench. She must've woken up.

"I'm Huiwon Jeong, by the way. Thank you for helping me this morning."

"Don't mention it."

Based on my first impression of her, I'd thought she was the frail, delicate type, but this was why you don't judge people by their looks.

"Sangah. Hyeonseong. Wake up. Why are you making faces like that?

This man risked his life to get this food. You weren't planning to eat it for free, right?"

Huiwon spoke her opinion with a straight face. No hesitation or mincing of words.

"Oh…"

Sangah's face turned red.

"That was shameless of me. I'm sorry. Of course we should pay… Yeah, I don't want free food, either. I don't like having to rely on someone else."

"I agree with Sangah. I'll start paying now, too."

I was surprised to see them react this way. *I suppose I shouldn't write off everyone in this apocalypse.*

"If you insist…okay. You know how to trade coins, right?"

"Yes, we learned a few days ago. Touch index fingers, and…"

"That's right. Now you just have to think of the amount you want to pay."

Huiwon, Sangah, and Hyeonseong each paid ten coins for a food item. I was glad that my companions were cooperative. *What I'm doing might seem a bit heartless now, but they'll eventually realize that this is the right decision.*

[A very small number of constellations are relieved you are not a complete chump.]
[A very small number of constellations have donated 100 coins.]

After all, this is the way to survive in this messed-up world.

[*Gilyeong Lee* has paid you 20 coins.]

"Huh? I think you paid ten extra."

"It's for the chocolate bar I ate earlier."

Gilyeong replied like it was the most natural thing in the world.

[A very small number of constellations show interest in incarnation *Gilyeong Lee*.]

Perhaps the ones who adapt the fastest to a new world aren't adults, but young children.

Hyeonseong, who was munching loudly on an energy bar, asked, "Are you going to be with us from here on, Dokja?"

"Ah, that…"

"Mr. Dokja Kim."

That wasn't Hyeonseong's voice. I turned around to see the major group standing behind me, with Inho Cheon in the lead.

I see. It was about time.

"Can I talk to you for a second?"

Cheolsu Bang, who was missing all his teeth, glared at me. When I narrowed my eyes and glared back at him, he looked away and pretended not to notice. *A small fry through and through.*

"Fine. Let's talk."

Inho nodded, satisfied with my response.

"Would the rest of you give us some space? I'd like to talk to Mr. Dokja Kim alone."

"Oh, I see…"

"No, no one needs to leave. Let's all hear what he has to say."

My companions, who had been getting up to leave, froze awkwardly. Inho's eyebrow twitched.

"Hmm, is that what you want? Well…it doesn't matter."

He was trying to play it cool, like he didn't care if others listened in. He wiped off a bench and plopped down. Two Cheoldu Gang members stepped forward on either side of him to hand him a cigarette and light it up. *Somebody's watched too many movies.*

"You don't seem like the talkative type, so I'll get straight to the point."

"Go ahead."

"Join our group."

I knew it.

"Someone of your caliber… I can offer you an important position. Help me lead the whole group."

"Why me?"

"I'm sure you know why."

Inho glanced at the wounded Cheoldu Gang members.

"You're a hero who saved the people from monsters. And every hero needs a position that fits their stature."

What an interesting thought. *So that's how he wants to use me.*

"And if I refuse?"

"Refuse? Interesting. I'd never considered that option."

Inho blew smoke right at me and smiled.

"Mr. Dokja Kim, this is not a request. With the power you possess, you have a responsibility. Can't you see the poor lost flock that needs you?"

People with dirty faces glancing at us surreptitiously. A child crying from hunger, and the elderly who looked about ready to collapse.

"I'm not asking for much. Work with me, for the sake of everyone's survival. You have the power to do that, don't you?"

"What exactly do you want from me?"

"We need a hit man."

Hit man?

"We had a person who performed that role until a few days ago. He supplied food by himself and taught us how to hunt in the tunnel to Yaksu Station. Well, to be exact, we spied on him as he did."

It was obvious who he was talking about. Junghyeok Yu.

"But last night, he suddenly left."

"So you need someone to replace him, huh?"

"Well, you've proven your ability by doing *that* to Cheolsu."

I saw Hyeonseong's and Sangah's eyes widen at Inho's words. They'd finally realized the truth of my entry into Geumho Station.

"You don't stand to lose anything, Mr. Dokja Kim. You'll be a hero to the people here, and one of the leaders of our group. You'll be well liked by everyone and—"

"I'm sorry, I'm not suitable for such a responsible position. I won't be joining your group."

"Hmm. Do you really think so?"

"Most importantly, I disagree with how you run your group."

I looked around at the Cheoldu Gang members, who looked like they were doing quite well, then at the people in the minor group, who were visibly malnourished and exhausted. Huiwon was glaring at Inho like he was her mortal enemy.

"Is that so? There isn't much I can do, then. If you change your mind, come see me anytime."

"That won't happen."

"Ha-ha. We'll see about that."

It didn't take very long to see what Inho had meant by that. Once the Cheoldu Gang had gone away, the ones who'd been hanging back came forward. People of the minor group. They immediately started yelling at me.

"Hey, we heard the rumors."

"Is it true you're hogging all the food?"

"There's barely enough to go around! How selfish can you be?!"

"I heard everyone worked together to get that food. What gives you the right?"

"Let Inho handle the food! Distribute it equally!"

I realized what was going on. I saw Inho watching from the back with a smug grin. His lips were moving.

"Your choice."

Share the food and become a hero…

…or keep it and become a villain.

If I chose the former, I'd be playing right into Inho's hands. Once I shared the food, I'd have to go looking for more with the members of the major group…until the day they inevitably betrayed me.

On the other hand, if I decided to keep the food, I'd become a public enemy and ostracized.

[A small number of constellations perk up.]
[Constellation *Secretive Plotter* scoffs.]

As people got riled up, Inho stepped forward.

"Now, now. Calm down, everyone. I think there's been a misunderstanding. Mr. Dokja Kim isn't like that."

Oh? He's working the crowd?

"Mr. Dokja Kim has agreed to work with us. We'll distribute the food equally. And he promised he'll cooperate—"

Inho spoke like he knew I'd end up joining him. I couldn't take it anymore.

"Stop."

I thought about it for a moment. *What would Junghyeok do? ...Oh, I see.* His absence was the answer to that question.

But I wasn't Junghyeok.

"Of course I'll share the food."

I saw the corners of Inho's mouth curl up. But he was celebrating too soon.

"But not for free."

I won't abandon everyone and leave like Junghyeok, but that doesn't mean these people are my responsibility.

Food would be given, but not for free. Everyone looked puzzled as if they didn't understand those words.

"What do you mean? Not for free...?"

"I'll keep it simple. I don't plan to monopolize the food. But I don't want Inho and his people to handle it, either. I'm not doing this for charity, and I don't trust those people."

I smiled and pointed at Inho Cheon.

"I'd like to trade with you. I'll sell the food to you for a fair price."

"S-sell the food?"

"What the...?!"

"H-how much...? You want money?"

I saw Inho's face darken. I smiled for him and continued.

"No, I only accept coins."

* * *

A few moments later, everyone had left except my companions from the minor group.

"Um…Dokja. Was that really the right decision?"

"Hmph, there's no such thing as a free lunch, Dokja. Good job. That was so satisfying."

Hyeonseong sounded concerned, while Huiwon seemed pleased.

Other people had turned their backs on us after I'd declared that I was selling the food. They were probably disappointed.

"I agree with Huiwon. The people here are too used to doing as the major group says."

"That's right. Those bastards…they have the entire station in the palm of their hand. People here just eat what's given to them like livestock. Then they're assigned recon duty and are forced to go out there like lambs to the slaughter. That's what happened to me this morning."

Huiwon shuddered. The ones who really monopolized the food were the major group, not me. Under the pretense of "fair distribution," they controlled who did or didn't receive rations, and used that to groom people to obey them.

Humans are weakest when they believe they're under protection. Once they perceive someone as an authority figure, they grow reliant and obedient without even realizing it.

"I agree. That's why I think your declaration was very meaningful. People need to have the will to solve their own problems. But…"

We followed Hyeonseong's gaze to the bags of food.

"…no one's bought anything. Maybe fifty coins per item is a bit steep? How about charging everyone ten coins like you did us…?"

I understood why Hyeonseong thought that way. People glanced expectantly at the major group but showed no signs of coming toward us. They needed more time. I replied calmly, "Let's wait and see."

Night fell. I could hear the footsteps of the giant monsters aboveground.

Some people talked in their sleep like they were having nightmares. Gilyeong and Sangah fell asleep first, and Huiwon was beginning to nod off.

"You should get some sleep, Dokja. I'll keep watch."

"That's okay. You go to bed first."

"But you must be tired."

"I have things to do."

"What do you mean?"

I pointed past Hyeonseong. Surprisingly, there were shadows approaching from the dark. Not just one or two, either.

"Um...are you still selling food?"

Finally, the people had started to make their move.

4

Most of the food I had was gone by morning. Huiwon shook an empty plastic bag in disbelief.

"What the heck? You sold everything overnight?"

"Yes."

"Hah! What a joke. Those two-faced cowards…"

"It wasn't just members of the minor group who bought the food, though."

They weren't the only ones who'd visited me in the middle of night.

"Mr. Dokja Kim, you've made the worst possible choice."

Inho Cheon had been among those people as well.

"You'll regret this."

The major group had bought more than half of the food I had. Of course, I'd charged them full price.

Huiwon was furious after hearing that.

"Wait. That means the major group has a monopoly on food again!"

"I guess so."

"How could you do that? Wasn't it your plan to encourage people to trade with each other and weaken the major group's hold over them?"

That was pretty sharp of her. I was a bit impressed.

"Yes, I was hoping the people would rise up on their own."

"Then you shouldn't have sold any food to the major group! Now it's back to square one!"

"Not quite. I made a lot of coins."

"What?"

A whopping 1,450 coins.

Not bad for one night of sales.

"Uh…what is Dokja thinking? Sangah, can we really trust this guy?"

Sangah flinched when Huiwon suddenly turned to her, then she smiled.

"I trust him."

Yeah, no pressure at all.

"Dokja, at the very least, you saved some food for yourself, right?"

"Nope, I sold everything."

Huiwon's jaw dropped. Just then, something poked my cheek. I turned my head to find a stick-shaped cookie pointed at me.

"Hmm? Is that for me?"

Gilyeong nodded his little head. *How cute.* I took the snack and put it in his mouth.

"I'm okay. You eat it. Oh, and speaking of food…you still have the stuff you bought from me yesterday, right?"

"Yes, I do."

"Me too. I have a little bit left."

"Why? You wanna buy it back? It'll be expensive, you know."

Huiwon jokingly shook a biscuit in the air.

"No, you should eat the rest of it now."

"Huh?"

"Make sure you eat it all by the end of the day. Don't leave any."

I repeated myself for emphasis.

"If you don't, you'll regret it."

"Why? …No, wait. Sangah, what're you doing now? Why are you listening to him?"

"If Dokja's saying that, then there must be a good reason."

Sangah opened up her last package of biscuits and began quietly munching on them. Hyeonseong looked confused but took out his as well. Gilyeong had already shoved everything into his mouth as soon as I'd spoken. *Good kid.*

"Ugh, I dunno about this… I think I'll save this one."

"I won't stop you."

I shrugged at Huiwon's reluctance. *It's her loss, not mine.*

Around lunchtime, the major group made an important announcement. People gathered around the center of the platform to hear Inho speak.

"We'll be limiting food rations starting from today. Each person will get three biscuits. And…"

Before he'd even finished, people began to clamor indignantly.

"What? Three biscuits? You expect us to live on that?!"

"But the recon team gets way more food than that! You think we don't know?!"

Inho smiled calmly at the angry crowd.

"You make a great point. It's true that those on recon duty receive more food. If you want that, then I suggest you volunteer."

"But most people who go out never come back! It's always just the Cheol-du Gang members who survive!"

"Are you telling us to go out there and die?!"

This made the people even angrier, but Inho remained calm.

"Those people were just unlucky. As you know, it's dangerous out there. If you have a problem, then how about getting the food yourself?"

"B-but…"

People suddenly grew quiet. Everyone knew that going outside meant certain death. Inho spoke up again, switching to a more appeasing tone.

"Ah, there's actually another way for you to get more food without joining the recon team."

"What's that?"

"By trading. Offer something that has value, and we'll give you food in exchange. Each person has a different thing they can offer, right?"

A number of people flinched as he stared at them coldly. They were the ones who had bought food from me last night.

[Character *Inho Cheon* has activated the skill "Incite" Lv.2.]

I wasn't surprised that he had the "Incite" skill. Most ringleader types had it, after all. The question is how they use it.

"I didn't want to resort to this, but Mr. Dokja Kim over there showed me something yesterday. He made a good point. There's no such thing as a free lunch, right? If you want food, you need to prove your worth. That's the fair thing to do, ha-ha. Thank you for opening our eyes, Mr. Dokja Kim."

That sly bastard...

Everyone's eyes were instantly on me. Most of them looked at me resentfully.

"It's all his fault..."

So this is how he's turning the crowd against me......

As I watched Inho disappear into his tent, I had a thought. Even this guy was nothing compared to the ones who would be at Chungmuro and Seoul Station.

There was already a crowd in front of the major group's tent. People were trying to barter for food.

"W-we'll pay with coins. How much is it?"

"Two hundred coins."

"What? But we don't have that kind of..."

"Then get lost."

Two hundred coins per food item. Even goblins would have been shocked by this price hike. A Cheoldu Gang member who was selling food in front of the tent spotted me and shuddered. Judging by the bandage around his thigh, he must have been one of the ones I'd beaten up when I first entered the station.

"Did I thank you yesterday?"

I turned my head to see Huiwon standing next to me.

"I think so."

"Well, I'll say it again. Thanks."

I wondered why she was here. Then I saw her eyes were fixed on the gang member with the injured leg.

"Over there. That bastard with the limp. He tried to force himself on me yesterday. I fended him off, though."

"...I see."

"Don't lay a finger on him. I'll kill him myself. You got that?"

The murderous gleam in her eyes was a sight to behold. It was surprising that she hadn't been chosen by a constellation. Had she awakened her attribute too late?

[Exclusive skill "Character Profile" has been activated.]

I was worried for a second after having activated the skill. This woman would be dead if I hadn't saved her. Would she be registered as a character?

* * *

<Character Profile>
Name: Huiwon Jeong
Age: 27
Sponsoring Constellation: None [Three constellations are currently interested in this character.]
Exclusive Attribute: Crouching Figure [Common]
Exclusive Skills: [Demon Slaying Lv.1], [Kendo Lv.1],
Stigma: None
Total Stats: [Stamina Lv.4], [Strength Lv.4], [Agility Lv.7], [Magic Power Lv.4]
Summary: As a crouching figure, she has incredible potential. Her attribute has not yet awakened, and therefore cannot be viewed.

* * *

Luckily, Huiwon's character profile was available. *I guess she's different from Sangah, Gilyeong, or Myeongoh.* Perhaps she was supposed to have a role in the story at one point, but the author had decided to scrap her character.

Anyway, she had quite an interesting attribute.

"Crouching Figure."

That name didn't sound like much, but it was one of the few hyper-evolutionary attributes in *TWSA*. Crouching Figure is a common-grade attribute, but depending on the circumstances of its awakening, it can evolve into a rare or even a legendary attribute.

Mad Butcher, one of the top one hundred fighters in *TWSA*, also evolved from Crouching Figure.

Huiwon Jeong.

I thought she was just a background character, but I should consider making her an ally. The fact that she had "Demon Slaying" worried me a bit, but if things worked out, she could grow into a powerful hit man.

"I don't know how you can be so calm, Dokja."

Calm… I guess it might look that way.

"You see, I've read a lot of novels, so I'm familiar with this kind of situation."

"Huh? That makes zero sense… Wait, where are you going?"

I didn't answer her and hopped down to the train tracks. Huiwon moved to follow me, so I offered her a hand.

"I'm good."

Huiwon waved me off, then jumped down next to me. We walked toward the tunnel going to Yaksu Station. I couldn't see much in the darkness, but there was a horrible smell. The stench of blood.

"You're not trying to go there, are you?" Huiwon asked. "Everyone who went that way died. Even the thugs. No one's come back alive."

She was wrong. Not everyone had died. I knew that at least one person had made it through and reached the next station.

We went back up to the platform. There was still a long line of people trying to buy food. Some objected to the main group and were beaten up, while others paid the unfair number of coins to buy the food. It was then that we spotted several young women from the minor group being sneaked into the back of the tent. Huiwon was furious.

"Ugh, seriously. Did you see that?"

"I did."

Inho had told people they could offer anything valuable in exchange for food. Those women were empty-handed. Huiwon gritted her teeth and stood up.

"I can't just watch and let them do this."

"What are you gonna do?"

"Stop them! I have to tell them that's not right!"

"So are you saying they should starve?"

"You expect me to just watch, then?"

"Yes, I think you should this time."

"What did you say?"

There was a hint of disgust in her voice. Instead of answering, I quietly watched. After a few minutes...

"...Sick bastards. They want us to do *what*?!"

The women stormed out of the tent, swearing in disgust. Thankfully, what Huiwon had feared hadn't come to pass. Just as I remembered from *TWSA*.

"Ha-ha-ha, come back anytime if you change your mind."

The rate at which people's ethics are eroded in the apocalypse varies from person to person. Just because they'd been forced to commit a murder didn't mean they'd become desensitized to all manners of crime overnight. Huiwon blinked in surprise.

"Did you...know that was gonna happen?"

"Yes."

"You had faith in those women?"

I didn't answer. I didn't trust people. I only believed in the novel I'd read. Huiwon continued, oblivious to what I'd just thought.

"I'm glad people still have some dignity—"

"For now, yes. It only means they weren't that desperate yet. Similar things will happen again once night falls."

Rumors of what had just happened spread throughout the minor group. Not only the women, but the people who were about to trade away their valuables eyed the major group's tent with distaste. It doesn't take that long for people to surrender their dignity in order to survive. Huiwon gnashed her teeth.

"I'll stop them next time."

"That won't solve the root of the problem."

"I know. But—"

"One of the women from earlier is a mother. If her child starves to death, will you take responsibility?"

Huiwon's eyes twitched. She looked down as if to hide her expression.

"Then…then what should I do? Damn it!"

[Character *Huiwon Jeong* has been influenced by your logic.]
[Character *Huiwon Jeong* is seized with a moral dilemma.]

I watched her wordlessly. The reason I'd taken the time to persuade her was to prevent her from acting impulsively.

A Crouching Figure with the "Demon Slaying" skill. If things went wrong, she could turn into an indiscriminate killer.

"Huiwon, the core issue here is food. This is happening all because one group is monopolizing all the food, right?"

"…Yes."

"So we remove the source of the problem."

"…Huh?"

I looked at the clock instead of answering her. *Should be anytime now.*

Bzzzt!

Yes, finally.

A familiar figure appeared in midair. Screams of fear everywhere. The instigator of this nightmare, who was ingrained in the people's minds.

Uhh… H-how have you been, everyone? I hope you're doing okay.

A goblin.

"Aaack! No!"

Most people had yet to grow accustomed to seeing their kind, so the goblin's appearance alone was enough to throw them into panic. A natural reaction, considering those bastards had brought nothing but bad news so far.

Even the fearless Huiwon flinched.

But more importantly…it wasn't Bihyeong.

Th-the one in charge of this channel has been disciplined... S-so for this scenario, I-I will be in charge.

Originally, Bihyeong had been the goblin in charge of the channel for this area. But the one in front of us looked different. Unlike Bihyeong's white fur, it was pitch-black.

A-anyway, it seems very p-peaceful around here. B-Bihyeong was bragging about it, but the scenario is way too easy...

"Why are you here? Just get to the point!"

Y-yikes! Don't get mad at me, everyone. I-I'm here for you guys...

"For us?"

"Th-then give us food!"

F-food? Ah-ha...food...

As if on cue, the goblin waved its hand.

[A penalty has been added to the scenario.]
[Food reserves are now prohibited.]
[All food reserves have disappeared.]

"H-huh?! What the hell?!"

People who'd been eating suddenly cried out.

All the food in the station was now floating up into the air.

H-heh-heh. Come on, now. This is no good. When a s-scenario starts, you should focus on clearing it.

Fsssh!

Canned food, cookies, energy bars, et cetera. All food reserves turned to dust and scattered in the air with a single wave of the goblin's hand. People fell to their knees, devastated.

Y-you can't sit here stuffing your faces, right? S-seriously, you e-earthlings are all trash...

The goblin's tone suddenly changed. I thought I remembered its name. There'd been a goblin like it in *TWSA*. It might have sounded timid, but this bastard was cruel even for a goblin.

From a distance, Inho looked at me with a stunned face.

Th-then please put on a good show, everyone. Heh-heh.

System messages followed.

[A penalty has been added to the scenario.]

[A new condition, Survival Fee, has been added.]

[From now on, a survival fee of 100 coins will automatically be withdrawn every day at midnight. You will die if you cannot pay the survival fee.]

[The survival fee is in effect until the second main scenario is cleared.]

I smirked wryly.

Now that's more like the TWSA *I know.*

EPISODE

05

The Warden of the Dark

1

Th-then good luck, everyone. Hee-hee-hee-hee.

With that, the goblin disappeared.

A food penalty and a survival fee.

I'd known about the first part. The second penalty was typical of *TWSA*, but it hadn't been in the original story. I could only suspect that my contract with Bihyeong had affected the storyline.

"Dokja, I'm asking you this just in case. Did you know this would happ—"

"Just a lucky guess. I was thinking about how the goblins could make our lives miserable."

"...You should become a fortune teller."

I gathered Hyeonseong and the others. It was time to make a move.

"Give back our food!"

"How...how could this happen?"

The people of the minor group were crying out in despair. Inho and the rest of the major group were also panicking. Inho bit his lip when our eyes met.

[Wait... Did he know this would happen? No, that's impossible.]

[You have accurately deduced character *Inho Cheon*'s thoughts.]
[Your understanding of character *Inho Cheon* has increased.]

...My understanding went up from that? I tried to guess other people's thoughts by reading their expressions, but I didn't receive the same message again. Meanwhile, Inho gathered the people to calm them down.

"Everyone, please gather around. I have an urgent announcement."

His announcement was simple. The situation had gotten worse, so he was going to enlist more people for recon duty. I was sure he was anxious, since there was no food left in the station.

"From here on, there will no longer be rations for people who don't volunteer."

Despite the severity of his statement, no one dared to object.

One by one, people hesitantly signed up for recon duty. Despite the disappearance of food, there was still hope in Inho's face. The more desperate the situation grew, the more power the major group would wield. Watching the scene with concern, Hyeonseong spoke up.

"Dokja, what should we do now?"

"We have to go get food, of course."

My companions tensed up. Getting food. That could only mean one thing.

"Should we join the recon team? We'll have to venture outside to get food."

"No. If we go aboveground, we'll die."

I looked at the gas masks lying on the ground. Those flimsy things would do little against the poisonous fog outside the station.

"But that's the only place we can find food—"

"Hyeonseong, the world has changed, and so must our diet."

I looked at the tunnel going to Yaksu Station.

"Wait, Dokja, are you saying—?"

"Yes."

Humans were no longer the apex predators of this world.

But that didn't mean we had to be prey, either.

"We'll hunt monsters."

* * *

A few moments later, my companions and I stood in front of the tunnel going to Yaksu Station.

"I see. You're going into the tunnels?"

I thought Inho would call us out for not joining the recon team, but it seemed he was happy to get me away from his little kingdom. He must've deemed me a threat to his power.

"Well, in the long term, I suppose we do need a team dedicated to clearing the scenario. You may go."

Sly bastard, talking like he's our leader. Well, it wouldn't be long before that smug look was wiped off his face.

[Your understanding of character *Inho Cheon* has increased.]
[Your understanding of character *Inho Cheon* has reached a certain threshold.]

Ah...I see. In order to increase my understanding of a character, I had to meet either of two conditions.

One, earn that character's trust or favor.

Two, accurately guess what they were thinking.

This time, it was the latter.

[Character *Inho Cheon* is suspicious of your intentions.]

Depending on my level of understanding of them, I was able to see their thoughts and feelings.

"Oh, right. Would you mind if someone from our group tagged along? We'd like to get some information about clearing the scenario."

I knew it. He wouldn't let us go without any strings attached. A familiar face reluctantly emerged from the back of the group. Of course, it had to be him. *Unlucky bastard.*

"D-do I really have to go with them?"

"Come now, Mr. Han, this isn't the time for that. You've been nagging me since last night that you wanted to make nice with Mr. Dokja Kim, haven't you?"

"Th-that's..."

The one joining us would be none other than Manager Myeongoh Han.

"Uh...Dokja, if you don't mind, can I...?"

"Sure. Come along."

My response seemed to surprise Myeongoh. He'd probably thought I was going to say no. Hyeonseong looked worried, but I had a plan.

Either way, we were ready to set out. Hyeonseong, Gilyeong, Sangah, Myeongoh, and me—in other words, the car 3807 crew had reassembled.

"Can I go with you guys, too?"

"...You haven't fully recovered yet. Are you going to be okay?"

"This is nothing."

And then Huiwon joined us, bringing our total to six. It could've been considered a small party or a large one, depending on how you looked at it.

Grrrr...

Not that it'd matter, considering what crisis awaited us.

[A new sub scenario has arrived.]

* * *

<Sub Scenario - Hunting for Food>
Category: Sub
Difficulty: E
Mission: Hunt and prepare a monster that can be used as food.
Time Limit: None
Reward: 500 coins
Penalty for Failure: ???

* * *

As soon as we stepped inside the tunnel, a sub scenario was triggered. Hunting for Food. A must-do sub scenario prior to the second main scenario.

> [A small number of constellations are looking forward to your performance.]

The tunnel was pitch-black before we were ten steps in. Even with flashlights, we couldn't see properly. It was evident that there was a barrier blocking the light. The real problem was beyond that barrier.

"Dokja, hang on. It's gonna get dangerous from this point on."

Huiwon, who was walking beside me, stopped.

"Walking in blind like this would be suicide. Besides, Gilyeong is here, too."

"Dokja, I agree with Huiwon. It's not too late. Why don't we send Gilyeong back? And while we're on the topic, the ladies should also..."

"Excuse me? I may not be as strong as you are, but I know how to fight, okay? I used to do kendo."

"Still..."

I interrupted them before this grew needlessly heated.

"Hyeonseong, I told you earlier. The world as we knew it has completely changed. There's no longer any reason to assume women are physically weaker, because anyone can get stronger by increasing their stats. And, Huiwon, by that logic, you're also wrong."

"...What do you mean?"

"Just like we shouldn't assume women are weaker, we shouldn't assume the same thing about children. Gilyeong, show them."

The boy stepped up. He sat down on the ground and stretched out his hand. Huiwon's eyes widened.

"Goodness, what is that?"

"Sh-shit! A cockroach?!"

Myeongoh freaked out. A cockroach skittered toward us, tethered to

Gilyeong's hand by a faint thread of light. Like a well-trained dog, the insect listened to Gilyeong's orders and disappeared into the dark.

"My attribute is Insect Collector."

Insect Collector. Gilyeong Lee had a rare talent that allowed him to communicate with insects through "Interspecies Communication."

"It says there's nothing up ahead. We should be safe for a hundred paces or so."

The rest of group looked astonished by Gilyeong's impressive reconnaissance. The boy continued with a confident look on his face.

"Thanks for the concern, but I'm not here to freeload on you grown-ups."

"Ah, right."

Huiwon nodded reluctantly. The boy scurried back to my side, and I patted him on the head.

I'd never seen the Insect Collector attribute mentioned in *TWSA*. Saving him at the beginning had been the right decision. We passed through the barrier and walked into the darkness inside.

[You have entered a dangerous area.]

"S-Sangah! It's dangerous, so hold my hand."

"...I think you're more scared than I am, Manager Han."

"N-no, I'm not!"

The air inside the barrier was heavy with humidity.

"Dim the light."

The flashlight didn't have a dimmer, so Sangah covered it with her hand.

"Urgh, please don't points the light down."

Huiwon gagged after seeing what was on the ground. Half-eaten corpses. The bodies of those who'd tried to move to Yaksu Station were strewn about. Sangah winced tightly, and Myeongoh shuddered. Even the fearless Hyeonseong looked shaken.

Surprisingly, it was Gilyeong who was most composed. There was no hint of fear in his face. His nonchalance made me feel a bit uncomfortable. *Does this boy think it's all some kind of game?*

"Some of these bodies aren't human."

As he'd said, there were other corpses on the ground, too. Monsters about the size of fully grown wolves. Their forepaws were shaped like a mole's.

The level-9 subterranean species, the ground rat.

The name made them sound rather harmless, but these monsters were like underground piranhas. They moved in groups, tunneling through the ground to relentlessly hunt down their prey. Dead ground rats were strewn about like the entire pack had been bombarded. Huiwon sounded incredulous as she spoke.

"Who on earth could've done this?"

Of course, there was only one person who could have done this to these ground rats. Junghyeok Yu. He had gone through this tunnel on his way to the next station.

It puzzled me. According to the novel, third-loop Junghyeok should've moved out of Geumho Station tonight or tomorrow. Why had he left earlier than he was supposed to? Was he in a hurry? What for?

"Dokja, can't we get meat from these to clear the scenario?"

"It says we have to hunt a monster ourselves, so probably not."

"Yeah, they don't look good to eat, either. On that note, how do we prepare the meat? Roast it over a fire?"

Roasting was good. The problem was that it had to be a special kind of fire.

"Never mind that for now. Huiwon, you said you were good at kendo, right?"

"Well, 'good' might be a bit of a stretch...but what're you doing?"

I began to use the Stone Hog's Thorn like a knife on the corpse of a ground rat. It was much harder than I'd imagined when I'd read the novel. But I eventually managed to skin its tough hide and cut out its spine. This was my first time doing this, so it got a bit scratched up, but it seemed to be serviceable.

"What's that for?"

"You need a sword, right?"

It may not have been as good as a Stone Hog's Thorn, but a ground rat's spine could be used as a weapon. If you fit the joints together in a certain way, it could turn become a trusty tool to get you through the early scenarios. Once I cut off the cartilage that connected the spine to the legs, it finally took on a proper shape. The result was a pretty good sword. I gave it to Huiwon.

"Thanks. It feels like we've gone back to the stone age."

"You'll have to sharpen the blade some more before it's of any use. Try grinding it with a rock or something."

"Hee-hee, got it, chief."

Huiwon seemed excited as she ground her new blade. Hyeonseong looked a bit envious as he watched.

"Should I make one for you too?"

"Oh. Can you…?"

"Everyone gather around. You might as well learn to do it yourselves. I'll show you."

I said that, but this was also my first time. I wouldn't have been able to do it at all if *TWSA* hadn't included detailed descriptions of using monster parts.

Why had *TWSA* been such a flop? The answer was simple. The author was way too obsessed with writing these meticulous details.

"…Dokja, for your first attempt, these weapons are surprisingly good."

We squatted down and made weapons together. Spears rather than swords this time. Since the rest of the group didn't have the "Kendo" skill, I thought spears would be easier to use thanks to their long reach.

I gave Hyeonseong the one made from the largest spine, and average-sized ones to Sangah and Myeongoh. For Gilyeong, I crafted a mace-like weapon made from the skull of a young ground rat.

[You have successfully fashioned your own weapons.]
[A very small number of constellations are interested in humanity's primitive roots.]
[They have donated 100 coins.]

We all received the same messages this time.

"They give coins for this kind of stuff, too?"

"We take what we can get. You all have some coins saved up, right?"

"Yes."

"Leave just enough for the survival fee and invest the rest into strength, stamina, and agility. Otherwise, you won't stand a chance."

"Okay, understood."

After the preparations had been made, we moved forward. We had nearly gone the hundred paces Gilyeong had mentioned.

[Sub Scenario - Hunting for Food has begun.]

Ground rats crawled out from the dirt. I did a quick count. One, two, three… There were exactly thirteen of them. More than I'd expected.

Grrrr…

An invisible line formed between our group and the pack of ground rats. Once anyone crossed that line, the battle would begin.

"There're no fancy tactics here. It's our first time, and this may sound harsh, but realistically speaking, I don't expect all of you to make it."

"What…?"

"But still, try to survive, everyone."

Myeongoh was the only one panicking. The rest of the group looked nervous but determined. The look in Huiwon's eyes, especially, was a sight to behold.

"Fine. Let's do this. We're all getting out of this alive."

Just as Junghyeok had tested me, I had a certain level of expectations for these people. One did not survive on determination alone in this world, even with a great adviser.

Eventually, you had to save yourself. They needed to realize that now.

"Let's go!"

And I'll find out who among these people I should take with me.

We took one more step forward, and the ground rats made their move.

The battle had begun.

2

Everyone fought well. To be honest, I was a little surprised.

Without being told to, Hyeonseong stepped up to the vanguard next to me, with Huiwon close behind. This naturally shaped our group into a solid formation—the three of us in the front, and the other three in the rear.

Less than one minute passed, but by then, the ground was strewn with the corpses of monsters with their necks pierced. Hyeonseong took down another ground rat and wiped sweat off his brow.

"…I think we're doing all right."

Once our overall stats are raised, humans are not weak by any means. Even so, Hyeonseong's willpower was exceptional. The average person wouldn't have been so casual in their first fight against monsters. There was a reason why he would later be called Steel Blade.

But the one who surprised me most was Huiwon.

"These monsters have a pretty simple attack pattern."

She was proving that her "Kendo" skill wasn't just for show. Each time her blade met a ground rat, a limb or its tail went flying through the air.

"Hiiyah!"

Huiwon had invested most of her recently earned coins on her strength stat. Her endurance left a bit to be desired, but each one of her strikes was forceful.

Shunk!

Just as I was having that thought, her sword cut an arc through the air.

"Damn it, I missed one! Can you get it?!"

Her voice was shaky like she was out of breath. Since her stamina stat was low, she was not suited for a prolonged fight. That was probably her only weakness.

Grrrr!

A ground rat dashed into our ranks, ignoring our blows. It was a devious move. Having scattered our formation, the monster did what every predator knows how to do by instinct: It lunged at the weakest-looking member.

"I got it."

But unfortunately for the ground rat, it had chosen the wrong target.

Whack!

Gilyeong gripped his weapon tight with both hands and slammed it down on the monster's head. Due to his small frame, the blow didn't have the power to kill, but he had done enough. The rest of us could finish the job.

Pshk!

Sangah's sharpened spear pierced the ground rat's body. The monster flailed violently in an attempt to shake it off. Sangah looked panicked, but she maintained a tight grip on her weapon.

Kreee…

The ground rat ran out of energy and slumped. To be honest, I'd expected Sangah to have trouble adjusting, but she had proven me wrong. Most people would have seized up with terror like Myeongoh over there.

"U-ugh…!"

Myeongoh was busy hiding while the rest of us were fighting hard. But he couldn't even do that properly, and his shin was bleeding from a monster's attack.

Kreeek!

Once I'd stabbed the last ground rat with my thorn, it finally became quiet. I shook the blood from the thorn and checked on the group. Other than a few scrapes and bruises, no one was seriously injured.

An impressive first victory. Sangah and Gilyeong plopped down on the floor, and Hyeonseong stuck his spear in the ground to wipe his brow.

"…Dokja, how many did you kill by yourself?"

"Four."

"Tch, I only got two."

"Three here."

Watching Hyeonseong raise his spear confidently, my pride was a bit hurt. Only one fewer than me? I wasn't going all out, but still… I peeked at Hyeonseong's character profile.

* * *

<Character Profile>
Name: Hyeonseong Lee
Age: 28
Sponsoring Constellation: Master of Steel
Exclusive Attribute: A soldier who turned a blind eye to injustice [Common]
Exclusive Skills: [Bayonet Lv. 2], [Camouflage Lv. 1], [Patience Lv. 2], [Justice Lv. 1], [Weapon Proficiency Lv. 2]
Stigma: [Great Mountain Push Lv. 1]
Total Stats: [Stamina Lv.12], [Strength Lv.9], [Agility Lv.9], [Magic Power Lv.6]
Summary: This character's attribute is nearing evolution. He has quite a bit of trust in you. His sponsoring constellation is wary of you.
*A "Starter Pack" is currently in effect.

* * *

Huh, a starter pack? No wonder he's so strong. Master of Steel must've taken quite a shine to Hyeonseong.

The Starter Pack was a coin package that could be used by incarnations whose stat points were below level 10. It not only raised each stat by one but also granted the skill "Weapon Proficiency," making it useful in the early levels.

Hyeonseong was very lucky. Never mind a starter pack—most

incarnations were thrust into danger with no support from their sponsoring constellations.

"Dokja, you don't look so good..."

"Ah, no. I was just thinking about something."

Must be nice... It's not like I don't have the money to buy one. I just don't want to buy it. It'd be a waste, since my average stats are well over ten already. Damn it, if I'd only gotten access to the Goblin Shop a bit earlier...

"Let's gather all the ground rats we killed. We need to prepare food for today."

"Hmm... So how do we cook this? I don't think we should eat it raw."

"We can't eat it now, but there should be a way."

Did I sound too matter-of-fact? Everyone suddenly went silent. Hyeonseong was the first to speak.

"Dokja, I've been meaning to ask..."

"Yes?"

"Do you...know something about this whole situation?"

It was only then that I realized I'd slipped up.

"That's..."

I thought of regressors in novels I'd read, then about Junghyeok Yu. *So this is how they must feel when their secret is in jeopardy.* How would they respond in this case? I remembered a few options. I could try to convince them it was just a hunch, or come up with a lie like the one I told Junghyeok back on the bridge.

[Constellation *Secretive Plotter* is looking forward to your choice.]
[A small number of constellations are looking forward to hearing your answer.]

But, as a reader, I daresay the best response is...

"G-gaaah!"

...to make it so that I don't have to respond.

[Constellation *Secretive Plotter* nods in approval.]

"One's still alive!"

Huiwon screamed. Hyeonseong jumped to his feet. But the ground rat that had been hiding moved faster than anyone. It was also much bigger than others.

Grab—

"H-help meee…!"

It grabbed Myeongoh's leg and dragged him into the hole it had come from. Sangah, who was next to him, tried to swing her spear, but Myeongoh made the situation worse by clutching her body in panic.

"Grab onto this!"

Hyeonseong offered the handle of his spear, but it was too late. The ground rat had vanished underground, taking the two of them with it.

[Constellation *Prisoner of the Golden Headband* is furious about the predictable cliff-hanger.]

Huiwon was livid.

"Ugh, seriously… I knew that guy was nothing but trouble…"

"…I'm sorry. I was too slow."

Hyeonseong sounded despondent. I patted him on the shoulder to console him.

"There was nothing we could do."

"Should we go after them?"

I stared at the hole the monster had disappeared into. It was no ordinary hole. I could sense something on my skin. It was like the darkness had mixed into the air.

I pretended to think and quietly stepped back to turn on my phone.

The battery was at five percent. I'd traded some food to someone in the minor group in exchange for charging my phone this much.

[Your reading speed has increased due to your exclusive attribute.]

It didn't take long for me to find the passage I was looking for.

...Ground rats live in the deepest part of the dark fold, a sort of a subspace emanating from dark roots, a tree of the demonic realm. Ground rats breathe in the black aether instead of air. Thus, they can only live near the dark fold...

I knew this already, but it was worth reviewing.

I see. This is the entrance to the dark fold.

I read the rest of the passage, then put my phone back in my pocket.

"Dokja?"

Hyeonseong was looking at me anxiously. I nodded.

"We're going in."

"Oh, then…"

"But it'd be too risky for all of us to go. You and Huiwon should stand guard here. I'll send you a signal if something goes wrong."

Huiwon was shocked.

"No way… You're going in there with just Gilyeong?"

"His ability will be helpful for tracking down those monsters."

As she was about to strongly object to my decision, I gestured to Hyeonseong.

"Huiwon is in bad shape, so please take good care of her."

It looked like Hyeonseong had come to a realization.

"Understood."

"Hang on. I'm really fine, though."

"Huiwon, being confident is good, but you shouldn't be reckless."

"……"

She looked like she was out of breath. Clearly, she hadn't healed completely from the poisonous fog.

I left those two behind and ventured into the hole with Gilyeong. The shaft extended downward at a nearly vertical angle, but as soon as we entered, we could walk down somewhat normally, as if the direction of gravity had shifted. This was due to the magical energy emanating from the dark fold.

"This way."

We couldn't see a thing this deep in the darkness. I was only able to move forward thanks to Gilyeong holding my hand. Because the black aether absorbed all light, flashlights were useless. If it weren't for his "Interspecies Communication," I would've had to spend more coins.

"Uh, Dokja." Gilyeong broke the silence. "You did that on purpose, didn't you?"

"...Did what?"

"When the monster went for Sangah and the old guy, you let it take them."

I paused for a brief moment. The boy's hand now felt strange in the dark. Even before I could ask him how he knew...

"I know 'cause I was watching your face."

I couldn't believe he'd been observing me during all that. Scary kid. *No point lying to him. He's way too sharp.*

"You're right."

Messages came as soon as I answered him. The constellations must have thought this was interesting.

[Constellations of the absolute good alignment frown at your cruelty.]
[Constellation *Secretive Plotter*'s eyes glint in anticipation of your scheme.]

"Why did you do that?"

"I did it because of the ground rats' behavior."

I decided to answer him honestly.

"They have a habit of storing their catch in one spot. Sometimes, they not only hoard food but rare items as well. But it's like a maze down here, so the only way we can find the nest is by following their trail."

Gilyeong was quiet. I continued.

"I was expecting Myeongoh to get dragged off, but not Sangah, too."

"So your goal was the items all along? Not to save Mr. Han and Sangah?"

"That's right. Are you disappointed?"

"No."

I felt Gilyeong's little hand grab my finger tightly.

"You're not a good liar, Dokja."

"……"

"If you really were that kind of person, you wouldn't have saved me in the subway. I trust you."

I thought he was mature for his age, but a kid was a kid. He didn't know being mature and being an adult were two separate things.

[Some constellations get misty-eyed at this moving scene.]
[They have donated 200 coins.]

And this world was full of despicable adults who would take advantage of his "maturity."

The tunnel was longer than I'd thought, so we went down for quite a long time.

"Dokja."

"Yeah?"

"By any chance, are you a god?"

"…What?"

"Or maybe the 'main character'?"

Sometimes children ask the most acute questions. Perhaps it's because they still lack the ability to separate metaphor from hard fact. Gilyeong probably didn't know exactly what he meant by his own question.

"I'm not a god or the main character. In fact, I've always been jealous of the main character."

"But you do know something about this world, right?"

I debated for a bit before responding.

"I do."

"Then can I ask you something?"

"If it's something I can answer."

"Once I clear all the scenarios…will I get to make a wish?"

"A wish?"

That caught me by surprise.

"You know, there's usually a reward at the end of this kind of story. There's one at the end of this story, too, right?"

Gilyeong's breathing was shaking in the darkness. I suddenly remembered how he'd looked at his dead mom. People who adjust to the new world each have different ways of coping with it. Some descend into madness, while others turn to fanaticism. And some cling to irrational optimism.

"Yes, that's right."

I was glad it was pitch-black in here. This boy couldn't see my face right now.

"We're almost there, Dokja."

The black aether around us decreased rapidly. This meant that a dark root was nearby. I tensed up and pulled out the thorn.

[A small number of constellations hold their breath.]

I heard the sound of ground rats digging nearby. As the noise grew closer, my sense of the environment expanded. I could see a fire someone had made in the distance. Beyond the fire was a black chest. As soon as I was sure I was in the right place, the messages came.

[The sub scenario has been updated.]
[You have entered the ground rats' treasure vault.]

"Dokja! That's..."

Before Gilyeong could excitedly point out the treasure chest, I clapped my hand over his little mouth.

"Shh, wait."

The world of *TWSA* was ruthless. Constellations entertained themselves watching humans fight adversaries, and the obstacles in a scenario were designed to screw us over. If an enemy looked defenseless, like those ground rats, then chances were it was a trap. We couldn't even trust the system messages.

"Sometimes, there are things other than treasure in treasure vaults."

[Constellation *Abyssal Black Flame Dragon* is disappointed.]

Abyssal Black Flame Dragon...that bastard has wanted to see me dead for a while now.

Anyway, I waited. Soon, shadows began appearing near the chest.

Grrr... Squeak!

They were ground rats. They brought something through the tunnel and exchanged information by making odd crying noises.

Fwoosh.

As the number of ground rats grew, the number of flames brightening the area increased as well. Dark flames fueled by the black aether. The fact that they were burning all around us meant that we'd reached the center of the dark root, where black aether was overflowing. We heard some people talking.

"This is all your fault, Sangah!"

I'd have recognized that voice anywhere. Gilyeong seemed surprised, so I squeezed his shoulder firmly. It wasn't time yet.

"What do you mean, it's my fault?"

I could see the two of them being guarded by ground rats in the faint light. They were tied up with vines from the ground.

"I-if you hadn't gotten on the subway, I wouldn't be in this mess!"

"What does me taking the subway have to do with any of this?"

I can't believe Sangah's even bothering to respond to Myeongoh's nonsense. Is she a saint? Or is her sponsoring constellation Buddha himself?

"W-well…you always commuted on your bike, so I…"

Myeongoh blabbered on. There was a cold edge to Sangah's voice now.

"Wait. Manager Han, you were the one who stole my bike?!"

"C-come on! I offered to give you a ride in my car! You should learn when to accept someone's kindness."

"Answer me. Did you steal my bike?"

I suddenly understood what had happened. So this was why Myeongoh had been riding the subway instead of taking his fancy car.

Well, there were a lot of men who had their eyes on her—not only in our company, but around Geumho Station as well.

[Constellation *Demonic Judge of Fire* dislikes incarnation Myeongoh Han.]

Myeongoh's face had turned so red I could see it clearly even by the light of the dark flames. *This isn't looking good.*

"Fine! I did! So what?!"

"Why are you yelling at me? You're the one who took my stuff! That's theft!"

"Theft? None of that would've happened if you'd just gotten into my car!"

[Constellation *Prisoner of the Golden Headband* is tired of this pointless bickering.]

I was going to wait a bit longer, but I had no choice. I quietly readied the thorn.

"Look, Sangah. Did I harass you? Huh? It's not like I asked you out or anything! I simply offered to give you a ride home out of the goodness of my heart. But you kept refusing, so I—!"

I threw the thorn with all my might. It flew past Myeongoh's mouth and hit something in the dark with a whack.

"Gaaaah! Wh-what was that?"

[Constellation *Prisoner of the Golden Headband* is pleased.]
[You have received 100 coins as a donation.]

"Dokja!"

Sangah called my name. But I wasn't looking at them.

Craaack...

The darkness opposite the ground rats began to crack. *It's coming.* Of course that bastard had to be where a dark root was.

[A warden of the dark has appeared!]
[The sub scenario has been updated!]
[Sub Scenario - Defeat the Warden has begun!]

Ground rats cowered in fear like slaves before a king. A pitch-black figure appeared in the faint light. The monster reminded me of a grim reaper, but with tentacles on its back.

Gilyeong's face quickly turned pale.

"Ugh, Dokja, I—"

"It's okay, go ahead."

Gilyeong bent over and started vomiting. It was understandable, considering we could sense an incredible pressure from the warden of the dark, even from here. All the cockroaches near us were dead on their backs, having burst open from the presence of the warden. Gilyeong must've suffered quite a bit of mental damage since he had been connected to those insects.

"Gilyeong, how many more times can you use 'Interspecies Communication'?"

"...I can still do it once or twice."

"Okay. Stay here and rest for a bit."

I made him lean on the wall and then walked toward Sangah and Myeongoh. Myeongoh was in a panic and struggling to get loose.

"Ahh! What's that...?!"

I cut the vines wrapped around their bodies with my Swiss Army knife. I only used the weapon a few times, but it was enough to corrode the blade. That was the power of the demonic species.

"Stay back," I told the two of them as I picked up Myeongoh's spear.

The level-7 demonic species, warden of the dark.

Of all the monsters that had appeared since the apocalypse, demonic species were a bit special. The ground rats' treasure served as an offering to these horrors. Their kind was far more dangerous than other monsters of the same level.

[The warden of the dark is under the protection of the demon king it worships.]

"Kamun, Dehr, Etur."

Each demonic species has their own language and worships a demon king. They can draw upon their master's power through dark roots.

[The warden of the dark emits "Fear."]
[Exclusive skill "The Fourth Wall" nullifies the effects of "Fear."]

In other words, killing a member of a demonic species meant making an enemy of a demon king.

"Etur!"

I couldn't understand what it was saying, but this was bad. I really wanted to avoid fighting it.

"...Mother?"

It was Sangah's voice. Why hadn't she fled yet?

"I told you to stay back!"

"No, wait. That monster just said 'mother'..."

It was so unexpected that it took me a second to process what she'd said. *No, hang on.*

"Let's see... K-kardu emiren? Huh? Did I pronounce that wrong? Akedu?"

For a second, I thought I'd heard her wrong. But no, she was actually trying to speak to it.

"Kalidu!"

Surprisingly, the warden of the dark was nodding at what Sangah said.

[Character *Sangah Yu* has activated the skill "Interpretation" Lv.3.]

...No way. She's not only good at Spanish, but also demon tongue?

"So what is it saying?"

"Um...it keeps repeating—'become mother.'"

...Become mother?

The warden of the dark pointed at Sangah and yelled once again.

"Kalidu!"

Sangah blanched.

"W-wait, no! I'm not even married yet!"

The warden of the dark pointed at Myeongoh this time.

"Kalidu!"

Myeongoh, who had been wiping his bloodied lips, turned pale.

"Wh-why would I be a mother?! A father, maybe!"

A tentacle from the warden's back whipped through the air.

Swish!

"Urbff!"

Myeongoh's face began to turn black as the tentacle entered his mouth. Something went down his throat with a gurgling sound.

So that's what it means by "become mother."

I'd just remembered that demonic species impregnated other beings with their offspring.

"Sangah, you don't want to have kids yet, do you?"

"Of course not!"

Sangah understood what I meant and quickly stepped back. I swung the spear and cut the tentacle attached to Myeongoh. The monster cried out in anger.

"Kaliduuu!!"

Swoosh! Clang!

Little by little, its tentacles broke down the spear. Even the Stone Hog's Thorn, which had damaged the angler dragon's stomach, had begun corroding on contact with the warden, so this makeshift spear stood no chance.

Sangah had already dragged Myeongoh to safety.

She looked at me, as if asking, "We can beat this thing, right?"

But to be honest, I had zero chance of winning.

Swoosh! Swoooosh! Clang!

The spear was too damaged to use after it had parried just a few attacks from the monster. The hand I was using to hold the spear throbbed painfully. *This monster's not like the angler dragon back at the bridge—it's not meant to be fought and defeated.*

That was why I'd been planning to wait for it to leave, then open the treasure chest.

But every good plan has a contingency in case something goes wrong.

"Goblin! You're watching this, right?"

U-umm. Y-you knew?

The goblin appeared like a bright light bulb in the dark. I didn't know its name, but it looked like Bihyeong's cousin or something.

"There should be a package for me. Give it to me, quick."

Hee-hee. That's not m-my job. B-Bihyeong's in charge of that.

"And you're supposed to be filling in for him. Can't you see the constellations are getting impatient?"

[Constellation *Prisoner of the Golden Headband* is nagging Goblin Biryu.]
[Constellation *Demonic Judge of Fire* is threatening Goblin Biryu.]

Biryu let out a squeal, then gulped loudly.

F-fine, just th-this once. A-and only because it sounds f-fun!

The goblin mumbled something, and an item began to appear.

[An item has arrived from the auction house.]
[You have obtained the item Broken Faith.]
[The commission fee is waived due to your contract.]

Broken Faith. I had put the Angler Dragon's Nucleus up for auction through the Goblin Shop in exchange for it. And it had finally arrived.

"Keh."

The warden of the dark sneered at the item that had appeared in my hands. Understandable, since it was only a D-grade sword. Also, it was broken.

[This item is too worn out to be used. Its durability is too low for it to be effective.]

Even the goblin who'd given it to me was laughing.

Y-you thought you could fight with that? And you can't u-use it unless you have a very s-special skill anyway...

Of course, I knew that. If I hadn't, I wouldn't have traded for it.

"Haah…"

I took a deep breath and concentrated.

Vweem.

The sword was vibrating rapidly. Biryu was shocked.

Huh? H-how?!

Yeah, you'd better be shocked. After all, I purchased this skill from your friend for a whopping ten thousand coins.

A whitish-blue aether began surrounding the broken blade.

"White Star Weapon Aura."

After I'd killed the angler dragon, I'd purchased this skill from Bihyeong. Unlike the top-level martial arts skills, this one had a small penalty. But it was the most powerful weapon aura skill I could get right now.

[Broken Faith reacts to your magic power!]
[Blade of Faith has been activated!]

Soon, the blade glistened as a new blade emerged from the tip of the broken one.

Broken Faith. This sword's true power is revealed when it's imbued with a weapon aura skill.

Swoooosh!

Dozens of tentacles spawned and obstructed my view. Even with my stamina level, I couldn't bear the monster's attacks. I was afraid. But there was a chance of winning now. After all, Blade of Faith was an extremely effective weapon against demonic species.

Fsssh!

The blade of light cut through the tentacles like a hot knife through butter, disintegrating them upon contact. The warden of the dark cried out and withdrew its tentacles. I felt my mana draining quickly, but I remained calm.

Shunk!

I focused on wielding my sword. I missed a few tentacles because I didn't have "Combat Sense," and my technique was awkward because I didn't have "Blade Proficiency." *Naturally, since I'm not a swordsman. I'm a reader.*

And a reader should fight like a reader.

[Your exclusive attribute improves your memory of the pages you've read before.]

The pages of *TWSA* turned in my head. The scene I'd read over and over, the moves I'd fantasized about pulling off countless times. I calmly reviewed the novel's description of this fight.

> ...It's possible to control the warden of the dark's attack pattern. When striking its left ankle, a tentacle on the top right reacts first...
>
> ...And after two attacks in quick succession, there will be an opening...
>
> ...Its tentacles can regenerate, but it takes several minutes, so...

Read a lot and apply what you've read in real life.

"Kraaah!"

Several tentacles flew into the air, severed by my attacks, and the warden of the dark screamed.

Gilyeong was watching from the other side. The boy's eyes were full of awe. Unfortunately, I wasn't the god of this world or its main character like he wished. But there was one thing I was confident about.

"Kardu. Mien. Dehro."

The warden of the dark roared in shock as it barely pulled itself together. From behind me, Sangah interpreted without being asked.

"How…my attacks…all of them…?"

So that was what it had said. I answered casually, as if this was nothing.

"Wanna know how? I read a lot."

I knew this world better than anybody.

3

Perhaps I could have drawn this out.

[Exclusive skill "Bookmark" has been activated.]
[The second bookmark is activated.]
[Duration is shortened because your "Bookmark" skill level is low.]
[Duration: 1 minute]

A brutal showdown worthy of the phrase "yield my flesh to claim their bones." A battle to end all battles.

[The character's skill will only be partially effective due to your low understanding of this character.]
["Weapon Proficiency" Lv.1 has been activated.]

However, I didn't do that. To be precise, I couldn't. It took all my wits to survive from moment to moment, and all my energy to strike back. I pushed my muscles to the limit and clenched my teeth as I lunged at the mass of tentacles.

Shhk!

My surroundings zoomed by in a blur, and blood splattered onto my cheeks. An afterimage of a white flash, and a sensation of cutting through flesh.

[Your understanding of character *Hyeonseong Lee* has increased.]
[The second bookmark is deactivated.]

I felt thoroughly drained. That attack had taken everything I had. Soon, a shaky voice came from above.

...E-everyone, did you see that? I can't believe it...!

Biryu seemed to have forgotten its job in sheer surprise. Of course it was surprised.

[A small number of constellations doubt their own eyes.]
[Constellation *Abyssal Flame Dragon*'s eyes widen with shock.]

After all, the powerful level-7 demonic species was lying on its back like a dead cockroach.

[Constellation *Prisoner of the Golden Headband* pulls out his hair in satisfaction.]
[You have received 500 coins as a donation.]

Severed tentacles lay scattered all around me. The ground rats that hadn't been killed as collateral damage had long since fled. The warden of the dark was still alive, writhing on the ground. Its lips were twitching.

"...Keeh. Keeh. Keeh."

I wasn't anywhere near strong enough to fight a level-7 demonic species.

So I had prepared. I wasn't strong like Junghyeok Yu, nor did I have a good sponsoring constellation like Hyeonseong Lee.

[A constellation with OCD praises your preparedness.]
[You have received 200 coins as a donation.]

The only advantage I had was information. But information can be the greatest power in this world.

Zzzzt.

And the result of that information was the gleaming blade of light in my hands.

A-an aether blade? This early in the s-scenario...? Everyone, are you seeing this?

Thankfully, the goblin spared me from having to explain by blabbing all about it.

An aether blade. A main skill used by incarnations who are sponsored by top-tier constellations. Martial artists from Murim often referred to it as "blade energy."

"Actually, this isn't a true aether blade. The real thing is much more powerful."

Th-that's right! Technically speaking, Broken Faith absorbs magical power to project a blade, and you infused it with White Star Weapon Aura.

I guess Biryu was a goblin for a reason. It wasn't totally stupid.

This is crazy... What's with all these freaks in Bihyeong's channel?

As if on cue, Blade of Faith expired with a fizzling noise.

[The durability of Broken Faith has run out. This item cannot be used anymore.]

A shame, but it had done its job.

"I cleared the sub scenario, so hand over my reward."

Ugh, fine. H-hang on.

Biryu hurriedly input some sort of command into thin air, and a message appeared.

[You have fulfilled the conditions of the sub scenario.]
[You have obtained 500 coins.]
[A small number of constellations are impressed by your scenario.]

The reward was smaller than I'd expected. Understandable, since I hadn't killed the warden of the dark yet.

B-but aren't you gonna finish it off?

Biryu looked at me with excitement. I took a deep breath and glance at the warden of the dark on the ground. Then I spoke in the kindest voice I could muster.

"I'm against killing things."

A-against killing...?

"I don't take lives lightly."

[Constellation *Demonic Judge of Fire* exclaims that she knew it all along.]
[You have received 100 coins as a donation.]

Of course, that was a lie.

[Constellation *Secretive Plotter* gazes at you with a sinister grin.]
[You have received 100 coins as a donation.]

Biryu didn't know what to do.

B-but you'd get a huge reward for killing it. As the first person to slay a level-7 demonic species, you'd be awarded at least seven thousand coins! Th-that's a lot of money, you know!

"I said, I won't do it. Anyway, I have to open this treasure chest, so move—"

I brushed the goblin aside. It was true. The monster hadn't been my reason for coming here. So…

Stab!

[The level-7 demonic species warden of the dark has been killed.]

…*What?*

A look of malicious delight on the goblin's face, the warden of the dark dying on the ground, a sword made of ground rat bone sticking out of its body, and…

"Bwa-ha-ha-ha! I-I can become strong now, too! Dokja, you little shit! Didn't expect this, did you?"

Myeongoh was holding the sword as he cackled maniacally. It hit me what had just happened. Messages soon exploded in my ears.

[You are the first person ever to slay a level-7 demonic species!]
[You have achieved an impossible feat.]
[You have obtained 8,000 coins.]
[Contributors: Dokja Kim, Myeongoh Han]

Myeongoh must've gotten these messages, too. He'd probably received fewer coins, since his contribution was smaller than mine. Yet he was jubilant.

"You don't take lives easily? What a dumbass! This world is kill-or-be-killed! That's why people like you will never be on top! You underst—"

But would Myeongoh realize what he'd just done?

[The Demon King *God of Wrath and Lust* has learned of the warden of the dark's demise, as well as the identity of the one who dealt the final blow.]
[The Demon King *God of Wrath and Lust* will hunt down the one who killed his minion to the ends of the earth.]
[The Demon King *God of Wrath and Lust* will inflict a horrifying curse upon the incarnation who dealt the final blow to his minion.]
[Final blow dealt by: Myeongoh Han]

"Wh-what is this message?!"

Myeongoh was now screaming frantically.

[Constellation *Secretive Plotter* is impressed by your evil scheme.]

"Oh... Did I forget to mention? There's a reason why I didn't kill it."

[Constellation *Secretive Plotter* has recommended your scenario on Star Stream.]

Myeongoh stared into space in despair.

The Demon King "God of Wrath and Lust" was notorious for his curse that caused the victim's worst nightmare to come true. I didn't know what that would be, but something horrific would happen to Myeongoh.

I turned around to see Sangah and Gilyeong staring at me with their mouths agape. I smiled at them as if nothing had happened.

"Let's open up the treasure chest, shall we?"

* * *

A little while later, we showed each other what we had found after searching the treasure vault.

"I found something."

"Me too..."

[Mana Recovery Bracelet]
[Rusty Iron Shield]

Both were only D-grade items, but they were better than nothing. The Mana Recovery Bracelet would be useful to everyone, and the Rusty Iron Shield would be good for Hyeonseong. Despite its rather weak-sounding name, this wasn't a bad shield at all. After all, iron from another world was much stronger than iron from ours.

"A bit disappointing, to be honest," confessed Sangah.

Disappointing. She was right. Despite being a treasure vault, the area was quite empty.

Junghyeok Yu had probably stopped by here on his way to Yaksu Station, quickly grabbing the treasure to avoid a troublesome confrontation with the demonic species. That made us robbers stealing from a house that had already been cleaned out.

"It's okay, we still got the most important prize," I told Sangah while looking at the black chest in the middle of the vault. We opened it right away.

Inside was a brazier, if one could call it that. It was small enough to fit in my pocket.

[Mana Brazier]

Good thing it's still here. Actually, this was a key item in this sub scenario.

[This Mana Brazier is limited to one per incarnation.]

Junghyeok had probably taken one, so there would've been two braziers in total.

"…What is that?"

"Hmm, I think I can guess what it does."

I feigned ignorance as I lit up the brazier and put a dead ground rat's leg on top of it. The huge chunk of meat looked comical sitting on top of the tiny brazier, but within five seconds, there was an amazing transformation.

"Whoa, that smell…"

First came a delicious aroma, then the color of the leg turned brown.

"Meat!"

Gilyeong seemed excited. Sangah was quick to ask, "D-do you think it's safe to eat?"

"I'll try it first."

I grabbed the whole leg glistening with fat and took a bite. The juice that filled my mouth… I closed my eyes, forgetting to even chew. Reading about it in a book and actually tasting it were totally different.

[A small number of constellations are drooling.]
[A small number of constellations nod knowingly.]
[They have donated 100 coins.]
[Constellation *Abyssal Black Flame Dragon* smacks his lips.]

[Constellation *Prisoner of the Golden Headband* gnaws on his nails.]

...

There was a continuous flow of messages. Mukbang really is the best streaming content. I mean, who doesn't love a sumptuous meal?

"Go ahead. I think it's okay to eat."

As soon as I'd spoken, Sangah and Gilyeong went for the meat right away. They must've been starving, since they hadn't had much food in the last three days. Even Myeongoh, who had been lost in despair, had inched closer, eyes on the delicious-looking meat.

"U-um, Dokja, I…I'm not sure what came over me earlier…"

"Don't worry about it and eat."

"Thank you!"

"I mean, this could be your last meal, right?"

"Wh-what…?!"

Myeongoh turned pale. I'd said it in a jocular tone, but Myeongoh really was going to die. Not even Junghyeok Yu could escape a demon king's curse. Especially if that demon king was God of Wrath and Lust.

Each of us grabbed the leg of a ground rat. Here we were, munching on meat, mere minutes after a close brush with death. *I guess humans can't help themselves.* We all ate in silence. The flame of the Mana Brazier was calming and made me feel a little sentimental.

We kill something and eat it to live. That is the life of humans. That is how it's always been. But why did this feel different?

I looked up, and my eyes met Sangah's. She flinched in surprise, then spoke, her face contorted with distress.

"I'm so pathetic."

"…Sorry?"

"All I can do is gobble up the food you risked your life for… I couldn't help you at all…"

"No, Sangah. That's not—"

"But how do you know all this stuff, Dokja? Like, how to cook monster meat…"

"Um, that's…"

"Oh, is it because you read so many fantasy novels? All while I was studying Spanish… Much good that's doing me in this world."

I wasn't sure if she was being sarcastic. After all, most people wouldn't genuinely think that way. But when it came to the angelic Sangah…

"You were able to understand demon tongue thanks to your experience studying foreign languages. Your hard work is paying off, too."

"…Do you think so? Thank you for the kind words."

It sounded like she was being sincere. *Sometimes, I'm scared of what's going through this hard-working woman's head.* Sangah stared at the meat in her hand for a bit.

"I'm going to eat a lot so I can get stronger," she declared.

I gave her an encouraging nod and got up from my seat. Everyone was quite absorbed in their meals, and I took this opportunity to make my way to the back corner.

As important as the Mana Brazier was, it was not my main goal in coming here. I took a closer look at the black chest that had contained the brazier.

This is it. I'm sure.

Junghyeok had already taken the other Mana Brazier but couldn't have known the real treasure in this vault was actually the black box.

In the original story, Junghyeok didn't find out about this item until his sixth loop. *Who was it that first discovered it? Was it "Flying Fox"? Hmm, I can't remember it clearly.* My memory of that scene was hazy, but I recalled a passage like this.

> "You know those weird boxes in the early scenario zones? Well, I tried putting something inside…"

Just then, Sangah had been staring at me. She spoke through a mouthful of meat.

"Wha's tha box do?"

"Ah, so this is..."

She looked at the box and tilted her head. There was some strange writing on the box.

...Wait, there's no way she can read this, can she?

"Random...item box?"

Damn it.

Foreign language speakers are scary...

"Uh...ah...hmm. So this is..."

I panicked a little. Thankfully, Sangah spared me the awkward explanation.

"C'mon, try it out, Dokja!"

"...Can I?"

Gilyeong was nodding enthusiastically as well.

Sangah gave me the final push I needed. "Please don't mind us. All the items here should be yours. You earned it."

Well, they'd caught me anyway, so I might as well just open it.

"Thank you."

[A small number of constellations nod in approval of your decision.]

I took out the nucleus of a level-7 demonic species from my pocket. It was the one I'd gotten from the warden's corpse. Then I pulled out the expired Broken Faith. According to *TWSA*, it was easy to use this box.

> "...and who would've thought? It turns out those boxes are limited-edition premium items."

I put the demonic species's nucleus and Broken Faith in the box.

> "Haah, you don't believe me? I saw it with my own eyes. If you place a low-grade item in the box and close the lid..."

* * *

Actually, I didn't know what would happen when I put these two items in the box. But one thing was for sure—something amazing would come of it.

"...you're guaranteed to get a high-grade item!"

Soon, the closed box began to gleam with a dazzling light.

EPISODE

06

Time of Judgment (Part I)

1

Limited-Edition Item Box.

A coin item sold for a limited time during past scenarios in *TWSA*.

W-wait... Wh-what's that box doing here?!

Biryu had shown up a little too late and was in shock.

I-I thought we did a full product recall on those!

According to *TWSA*, this item had quite a complicated history.

It had been released for sale long before the scenarios began on planet 8612, before being forcibly recalled by Star Stream management. This was inevitable because the ability to put in a low-grade item and get a guaranteed high-grade item in exchange was way too powerful—enough to upset the balance of the scenarios.

Furthermore, the price tag on this ridiculous item was a whopping one million coins. Constellations had been furious about this blatant money grab, and the foolish goblin who had created it had been fired from management.

D-dear constellations, that's... I don't know why that box is—! H-hee-hee-hee-hee! End stream!

[Channel #BI-7623 has been shut down momentarily.]

Once Biryu disappeared, the constellations went silent as well. Too bad I couldn't hear their reactions to this nonsense. It must have caused quite a stir.

Vrrrr.

I looked at the vibrating chest. The random loot box was starting the gacha process.

[You have placed a sword-type item in the box. The reward will be of the same type!]
[Random loot gacha has begun!]

A limited-Edition Item Box spits out a high-grade item no matter what grade item is inserted. In other words, it could be anything from C-grade to SSS-grade. It was all down to luck.

[The item offered to the box is related to a certain constellation!]
[You have greatly increased the chance of receiving an item related to that constellation.]

...Huh? I hadn't expected that. But it didn't seem to be a bad thing. My clenched fists got sweaty. I'd never gotten this anxious, even when I'd paid for monthly gacha in an online game. *Please be A-grade or higher!*

[A high-grade item has appeared!]
[The box has 0 uses remaining.]

Finally, it stopped shaking, and the bright lights were dimming. I looked at Sangah and Gilyeong, whose eyes were twinkling with curiosity.

"Shall I open it?"

"Yes!"

We opened the box.

"Wooow!"

Gilyeong shouted so loud that it startled me. But even more surprising was what was inside.

An elegant-looking hilt and a pure white blade... It reminded me of Broken Faith somehow.

I looked up the item information right away.

* * *

<Item Information>
Name: Unbreakable Faith
Grade: Constellation Artifact
Description: The sword wielded by the hero Kaizenix, who led Grunciad into the golden age of magic in the past. It is imbued with Kaizenix's mastery of aether and can generate Blade of Faith with Fire, Dark, or Holy element.
As an added bonus, this item increases the user's stamina and strength stats by two when equipped.

* * *

I was speechless.

No way... Is this for real?

Not an alphabetically graded item, but a bona fide constellation artifact?

"D-Dokja! I can tell it's an amazing item just by looking at it!"

It was, indeed.

In *TWSA*, constellation artifacts are the only items which are excluded from the grade system. Not only because they have great power, but also because they are very special.

Every constellation artifact contains the power of a constellation when they were alive. Its ability varies depending on where the associated constellation was from and how well-known they were, but the simple fact that it contains a constellation's power makes it extremely valuable.

Additionally, this one increased strength and stamina by two. Items are rated A-grade just for granting one stat point, so this was S-grade at the very least for the stat bonus alone. Even Junghyeok likely hadn't acquired something like this yet.

I turned to Sangah and Gilyeong out of courtesy.

"...Is it okay if I keep this?"

"Yes, of course! It's yours."

Sangah answered enthusiastically. Gilyeong nodded energetically. I took a peek at Myeongoh, but he was munching on a ground rat's leg with a dazed expression while muttering to himself. I thought he would've spouted some nonsense about how he should get the item... *Weird.*

[You have obtained a constellation artifact.]
[The owner of the constellation artifact is curious about you.]

Based on that message, I assumed this constellation still existed somewhere. *I should look through* TWSA *later.*

"Let's start heading back. No need to take the meat. There are plenty of ground rats outside, so we just need the Mana Brazier."

"How will we get back?"

"With Gilyeong's 'Interspecies Communication'—"

But the boy didn't look well.

"Dokja, um..."

"Yeah?"

"There are no insects around here."

All the insects around us had been killed when I'd fought the warden of the dark. I hadn't considered this.

"Not even one? There should be some alive. If you use your attribute while we're on the move..."

There were so many insects in this world, so there should have been some left to communicate with. But Gilyeong looked worried.

"Actually, there's one I can call…"

He mumbled something, closed his eyes, and began concentrating.

"Dokja, something's wrong with him!"

The boy's eyes rolled into the back of his head. Blood dripped from his nose.

"Gilyeong?"

Suddenly, there came a loud thud followed by tremors from above us. Dust and dirt rained down from the ceiling of the tunnel. The vibrations were from aboveground.

I instantly had goose bumps all over my body.

"Gilyeong! Gilyeong Lee! Snap out of it!"

"Uh… Dokja?"

His eyes came back to normal.

"Gilyeong! Deactivate your skill! Now!"

That seemed to jolt him awake, and he stopped his skill immediately. Once the tremors died down, I breathed a sigh of relief. I remembered that the surface was teeming with incredibly dangerous monsters.

There was the level-7 monster plague rhinoceros I'd seen before entering Geumho Station. And I'd also spotted at least one monarch species insect of an unknown level. Of course, as the name suggested, a monarch species insect was also an insect.

"Sheesh…"

I was going to say something, but put my hand on Gilyeong's head instead. *I can't believe he can call on a monarch species insect… Who is he, Jean-Henri Fabre? We could've been buried alive.*

"Don't use that skill for a while unless I tell you to, okay?"

"Okay…"

Gilyeong looked a bit sullen. We had no choice but to wait.

"If we go into the dark fold now, we'll get lost. Let's wait until small insects return to this area."

It had been easy enough to enter, but the dark fold was a dangerous place. One wrong turn, and we could get lost for days without realizing. Sangah raised her hand.

"Um, if we're just trying to get back, I think I can help instead of Gilyeong."

"...How?"

I nearly blurted out, "Are you going to communicate with the dark fold this time?" But I stopped myself, because it would've sounded sarcastic.

"I have a similar skill," Sangah said reluctantly.

That reminded me. I still didn't know who Sangah's sponsoring constellation was.

"What skill is that?"

"One way to explain it is...it's a thread that shows the way you came..."

A thread?

"...Excuse me, Sangah, but may I ask what your attribute is?"

I couldn't read Sangah's thoughts because she wasn't a character from the novel, just like I couldn't read the thoughts of Myeongoh or Gilyeong.

"Um, it's..."

Sangah looked like she didn't know what to do. It would've been less frustrating if I could use "Character Profile" on her. I tried activating it one more time as a test.

[Exclusive skill "Character Profile" has been activated.]
[This person is not registered in "Character Profile."]

I thought so. But there was another message this time.

[Currently collecting data about this character.]

...Huh? I hadn't seen this one before. I just remembered that I'd heard a similar message when Sangah had activated her "Interpretation" skill. Originally, that message hadn't been there. By any chance, did "Character Profile" update as time went on? *No way...* This gave me quite a lot to think about, but reassuring Sangah came first.

"Sorry, I shouldn't have asked. You did the smart thing. Be careful about telling others your attribute from now on, too."

"Dokja, it's not that I don't trust you, I—"

It felt like Sangah was trying to tell me something. Suddenly, a thought occurred to me.

"Sangah, by any chance, did your sponsoring constellation say anything about me?"

She looked distressed and lowered her head.

"I'm sorry."

She barely managed to reply with her quivering lips. It looked like her sponsoring constellation had done more than just tell her about me. They had most likely sworn her to secrecy, on pain of death. I didn't know who her sponsoring constellation was, but they must've decided to give her their full support.

"It's okay. I understand."

"Thank you…"

No need to thank me. It's not like the only way to find your sponsoring constellation is from you… In fact, this made my heart beat with excitement. *Let's call it a reader's instinct to fill in the blanks.*

"I'll use the skill, then."

Shiny threads soon appeared from Sangah's fingertip and began to extend.

"Actually, I thought this might happen, so I spooled a thread."

One thread was connected to me, and another one stretched out to the tunnel. My guess was that the other end was connected to Hyeonseong or Huiwon.

"Let's get going."

There was no way Sangah had had this kind of skill from the start. It was probably a stigma from her sponsoring constellation. A thread that leads you out of a labyrinth… *Sounds like a constellation I know.*

[Channel #BI-7623 is now online.]

A message indicated that the constellations were coming back into the channel.

[A small number of constellations have filed a complaint about the channel's transmission system.]
[Constellation *Abyssal Black Flame Dragon* is curious about what came out of the random box.]

Heh, you didn't see what happened, did you? Well, too bad.

Damn it! What did that bastard do to my channel...? Ha-ha-ha! Hello, everyone. Did you miss me while I was gone?

Yeah, I kinda missed— I caught myself. *It's a voice I'm used to. That's all.*

It was Bihyeong.

* * *

...I see you've been up to even crazier antics while I was gone.

Am I the reason you were away?

Well...in a way, yeah. I got a warning from management for abruptly cutting off the stream and putting on ads for too long.

Only I could hear Bihyeong's voice. This was "Goblin Communication," which allowed their kind to talk to one another secretly. Of course, it was a violation of the rules to use it with me, an incarnation.

But I've decided not to sweat the small stuff. A few trips to see management aren't gonna kill me. By the way...how did you know about the random box?

I just knew.

Ugh, I can't believe you saw my greatest failure...

Your greatest failure?

......

...Wait, you were the one who came up with that absurd pay-to-win item?

Even I, the biggest fan of *TWSA*, hadn't known about that.

Damn it! I got way too greedy with that one...

"Wow, this is really yummy!"

Bihyeong's yapping was cut off by Huiwon's exclamation.

Ten minutes ago, we had reunited with the rest of our gang with the help of Sangah. Thankfully, Huiwon and Hyeonseong had guarded the barrier until our return.

"You'll feel better if you eat this."

"Mmm, I think I do already."

Huiwon tried stretching her arms, and I could clearly see that she had recovered from the poison. Ground rat meat has a detoxifying effect when properly cooked.

"Looks like you scored a bunch of items down there. Not just the Mana Brazier..."

"Guess I did pick up a few things," I answered, glancing at Hyeonseong.

For the last few minutes, he'd been trying on the Rusty Iron Shield I'd given him, carefully polishing it like it was brand-new car.

[Character *Hyeonseong Lee* feels slightly loyal to you.]

Huiwon looked at him enviously.

"Anything I can use?"

"Nope."

"That sword, maybe?"

"It's mine."

"You'll share the meat with everyone, right?"

"If they pay coins."

"...You really love money, don't you?"

"Let's say I love staying alive."

We bantered as we walked back to the station, carrying a cooked ground rat each. Before we knew it, we'd arrived at the end of the tunnel. Suddenly, it was bright, and I could see the people of Geumho Station. But something was off. Everyone seemed on edge.

[Twenty minutes remaining until checkout.]
[Please prepare to pay the survival fee.]

I realized what was going on after looking at the clock.

It's that time already?

I didn't know the word "checkout" could be so scary.

"Coins, please give me coins!"

"My kid doesn't have coins. Please, someone…!"

If they'd been diligent about clearing the scenarios, it wouldn't have been difficult to earn a hundred coins. But diligent humans are rare.

"I'll give you a million—no, ten million won! Who'll sell me one hundred coins?"

The price of coins was going up by the second.

How ironic. Currency which had no value before the apocalypse had a premium exchange rate. I spotted a group watching from the distance, sneering at the people's desperation. The ones who already had enough coins for the survival fee—Inho Cheon and the Cheoldu Gang.

A few women ran over to argue with them.

"B-but you said a hundred coins for one go!"

"Hmm, did I? I don't remember."

"What…?"

"Things have changed. How about a hundred coins for twice? Not a bad deal, right?"

The sound of Cheoldu Gang's laughter. I could guess what was going on. Huiwon had already pulled out her sword and was glaring at the gang.

"Sick bastards! I'll—"

[Character *Huiwon Jeong*'s attribute is about to evolve.]

It was almost time for Huiwon. This wouldn't be a bad time for her attribute to evolve but…it was a little too early. She needed to hold back for a bit longer in order to get the attribute I wanted her to have.

At that moment, there was a message from the system.

[Soon, the survival fee will be processed.]

"Help me! Help me!"

Each of my companions seemed to react differently. Hyeonseong looked at the ground in sadness. Huiwon bit her lip hard as she gripped her sword. Everyone here knew the price for not paying the survival fee. They'd experienced enough of the scenarios to know there'd be no mercy.

"…Dokja."

Sangah looked at me.

"Yes."

In this world, coins are power.

A person with coins can buy items and increase stats.

A person with coins can have it all.

[Some constellations have joined the channel following a recommendation.]
[Constellation *Secretive Plotter* awaits your decision.]
[Constellation *Prisoner of the Golden Headband* awaits your decision.]
[Constellation *Demonic Judge of Fire* awaits your decision.]

And right now, I'm the person with the most coins in Geumho Station.

2

As I was about to speak, I heard Inho's voice.

"Ah, Mr. Dokja! Good timing."

He looked happy to spot us. I had an uneasy feeling as he continued to speak loudly.

"If I recall correctly, you had quite a few coins… How many did you have again? I think you were the richest among us."

[Character *Inho Cheon* has activated the skill "Incite" Lv.2.]

People in the crowd hastily turned in my direction.

"C-coins?"

"Who has a lot of coins?"

Before long, everyone's eyes were on me. *What a sly bastard.*

"M-Mr. Dokja, right?"

"Please, help! I beg you!"

People ran toward me, gasping in desperation as they clutched at me. There were about twenty of them. If I handed out a hundred coins to each of them, I'd lose a whopping two thousand coins. But if I didn't, I'd become the most hated villain in Geumho Station.

[Your understanding of character *Inho Cheon* has increased.]

"Ha-ha, Mr. Dokja. Sadly, I don't have enough to help these poor people… But you have plenty, right? Are you just going to watch?"

I sighed to myself.

I'm done playing along with your games.

[Constellations of the absolute good alignment have deemed character *Inho Cheon* "Evildoer."]

I'd been patient with this scum for long enough.

"H-help me!"

"Help me, please!"

People cried out to me with the most pitiful expressions on their faces.

Ha-ha-ha! This is getting interesting! By the way, you have ten minutes left!

Bihyeong looked like he was having the time of his life, and my allies were helplessly staring at me. I slowly closed and opened my eyes and took a deep breath.

"I see. You want me to give out coins?"

Then I smiled.

"Why should I?"

I looked over the crowd.

The first scenario had been the original sin. No one here was innocent. They'd trampled other lives to save their own, only to squander their second chance by cowering down here and doing nothing.

"Wh-what do you mean, 'why'?!"

"You have a lot of coins! So it's your duty to share them with us!"

Inho burst out laughing at the chaos.

"Mr. Dokja, you never disappoint!"

"……"

"You've been like this ever since you came here. You even charged for the food you brought. Do you know how many of these people would be safe now if you hadn't forced them to pay in coins?"

"Yeah! Inho's right!"

"You thief…! Gimme back my coins!"

It was quickly turning into a kangaroo court, and I was the defendant. I'm sure this was Inho's goal all along.

"Everyone, please, calm down! You're being irrational…!"

"Dokja isn't that kind of person!"

Sangah and Hyeonseong tried to calm everyone down, but the crowd was out of their minds. And then, Inho threw a torch into the kindling.

"Mr. Dokja, I'll give you one last chance. Give back their coins."

"What if I say no?"

"Then I can't guarantee your safcty anymore."

A mob of around twenty people began to approach me.

"Y-you… Gimme back my coins!"

Yet no one seemed quite ready to make the first move. Eventually, a member of the Cheoldu Gang stepped forward impatiently.

"What're you waiting for? Kill him! Take the coins he has on him!"

The inciter was a man with a muscular frame. I activated "Character Profile" to check his information.

* * *

<Character Profile>
Name: Minsang Han
Exclusive attribute: Gangster [Common]
Total Stats: [Stamina Lv.8], [Strength Lv.8], [Agility Lv.8], [Magic Power Lv.2]

* * *

His stats were quite high for a petty thug. He couldn't possibly have started out this strong, which could only mean… *So* that's *what these bastards have been doing.* This guy had clearly let his high stats go to his head.

"Die, you little shit!"

Minsang swung a steel pipe. A deadly weapon powered by level-8 strength. The Dokja Kim of the past would've been paralyzed with fear, but…

Shhk!

Minsang's steel pipe clattered to the ground, along with the hand that was holding it.

"Gaaaah!"

Having tasted blood, Unbreakable Faith surged with a blinding white light. I quietly scanned the crowd in front of me.

"Uh-ughh…"

They had turned pale as a sheet, having witnessed me dispatching a thug of the Cheoldu Gang with a single strike. *That should've been enough of a show. Time to get to the real game…*

"How pathetic… Do you really think I'm the reason this is happening?"

I spoke slowly, gazing at each of them one by one. I spotted Inho's panicked face on the other side of the mob.

"You know deep down that I'm not the one to blame."

People opened and closed their mouths like dumb goldfish in a bowl. I continued.

"You're taking it out on me because you're scared of those thugs. You know exactly what the real problem is and why you're about to die, but those guys are stronger than you…"

"Ha-ha, you can stop right there, Mr. Dokja! What are you trying to—?"

"…because they have higher stats and more coins than you, so you don't dare stand up to them! But you know what?"

I stepped forward. The entire crowd moved back like startled goldfish. But they were already in my fish tank.

"Think about it. How did they get so strong?"

I moved one more step.

"Where did they get all those coins? Just because they're violent thugs? Of course not."

[The people are starting to get agitated.]

Even in the midst of their fear, there was a moment of clarity. Suspicion spread from face to face.

"C-come to think of it, how *do* you have so many coins, Inho…?"

"Ha-ha, you know why. I've sold this and that, and—"

"Do you really think you get high stats just like that? Really?"

Inho shut his mouth. I scanned everyone's faces once again from left to right as I spoke.

"When I first arrived at Geumho Station a few days ago, there were eighty-seven people here."

"……"

"How many people are here now? It looks like fifty at most. Do you know why?"

"Th-that's because people were killed by monsters during recon—"

"Monsters? Do you *really* believe that?"

"Then how…"

"Use your brain, idiot. How come none of the Cheoldu Gang members have died?"

The whole place went silent at once.

"And why did they come back strong?"

[Constellation *Secretive Plotter* nods at your deduction.]

"Th-that can't be—"

One by one, people exchanged looks. The Cheoldu Gang slowly began to back off. It was my turn to throw a torch into the kindling.

"They egged you on, saying you could get coins by killing me."

[Constellation *Prisoner of the Golden Headband* pulls out his hair in excitement.]

"But how did they know you can get coins by killing other people?"

"Y-you people… Inho! Did you really…?"

"Shut up! It's all a lie!"

As soon as Inho stepped back, the rest of the Cheoldu Gang pulled out their weapons. A collective groan came from the frightened crowd.

Ha-ha-ha! Seven minutes left!

I moved closer to the others as I spoke.

"If you have a shred of pride left, stand up and fight."

Blade of Faith blazed to life. Anger began to fill people's eyes.

"Take back what was stolen from you with your own hands!"

As if on cue, all the Cheoldu Gang members came at me at once. And I charged right toward them.

"Because that's the world we live in now!"

A bright white flash, and people screamed.

Someone yelled, "Damn it, he's right!"

"You sick bastards!"

People began making their moves. Everyone here had previously killed someone.

"M-mommy!"

"Come here, Dayeong! Hold this! Swing it like you did back in the subway!"

There was a child and his mom.

"You bastards!"

There was a middle-aged man, too.

"You son of a bitch!"

However, the Cheoldu Gang had similar numbers to the mob that had turned against them. And they were incomparably stronger, as a result of hunting their fellow humans and seizing their coins. It was shaping up to be a very one-sided fight. If I hadn't been there, that is.

Shhk!

In a moment, the Cheoldu Gang members who came at me lost their arms or legs. The sickening sensation of cutting through human limbs spread through my hands. The incapacitated thugs looked up at me.

"P-please spare—"

But before he could finish, someone lunged past me and stuck her sword into his pleading mouth.

"I told you I'd kill him."

[All conditions have been met for the evolution of attribute "Crouching Figure."]
[Character *Huiwon Jeong*'s attribute is about to evolve.]

Huiwon's body emitted a bright and beautiful light.

I nodded. It was time.

[Character *Huiwon Jeong*'s attribute has evolved into "Judge of Evil [Heroic]."]

Judge of Evil. The strongest of the three "judge" attributes had awakened.

[You are a major contributor to the evolution of the Crouching Figure.]

[From here on, character *Huiwon Jeong* will not hesitate to be your sword.]

"You can stand back now."
Huiwon's eyes gleamed with a dangerous light.
"Because these bastards are mine!"

[Character *Huiwon Jeong* has activated the exclusive skill "Time of Judgment."]
[Constellations of the absolute good alignment consent to the use of this skill.]
["Time of Judgment" has been activated.]

A bloodred aura surged around Huiwon's blade as it cut a ruthless arc through the air. With graceful and precise swordsmanship, she danced through the ranks of the Cheoldu Gang. Sprays of blood everywhere.

"Arghhh!"

It was a downright massacre. Of course, it wasn't just Huiwon fighting. Sangah, Hyeonseong, and even Gilyeong were holding their own. But no one fought as hard as Huiwon.

She killed and killed again like she was born to slay. I cut a thug's arm, and she ran her blade through the heart. I cut another's leg, and she sliced off his head.

Huiwon finished off each and every one for me, no hesitation in her swordplay, as if she had been waiting for this moment.

"..."

Our surroundings were drenched with blood.

In the blink of an eye, Inho was the only remaining Cheoldu Gang member. And even he was gushing blood from wounds inflicted by the people he'd been lording over. Huiwon looked at me and I nodded. Inho bared his teeth in a malicious smile.

"Heh...heh-heh... Dokja Kim, you—"

But he was not allowed to finish. Huiwon had come up behind him and brought down her blade in a straight line, from the top of his head all the way to his chin.

[Every constellation in the channel feels an intense catharsis.]

With that, everyone stopped moving.

The battle was over.

But it hadn't hit anyone yet.

Just a short while ago, we'd been roasting meat and joking around, but that felt like a distant dream now.

In this damn scenario...

...Sangah was crying...

...Gilyeong closed his eyes...

...Hyeonseong bit his lip so hard that it bled...

...and Huiwon had slumped down in a pool of blood, having spent every ounce of her strength.

Yes, this was the reality of the new world.

[Survival fee is being processed.]

The sickening sound of bursting heads came all around the station.

Those who had the coins survived and those who didn't died. None of us could save anyone.

I faced them and stared straight into their eyes.

"Get up, everyone."

I looked up, but there was no sky down here. And yet, I glared up at the invisible sky, as if in defiance of some vast, inexorable destiny.

"The scenario has only just begun."

As the others got to their feet, I alone thought about the next scenario. Like turning a page, moving on to the next chapter. I felt only calm focus.

I had gained everything I should have from Geumho Station.

The next stage was Chungmuro.

Omniscient Reader's Viewpoint will continue in Volume 2.

AFTERWORD

The first thing we did before we wrote the afterword was argue if we should write it in the polite form or in the informal form. Sing liked the polite writing form, but Song felt embarrassed about writing in it. Our opinions differed. Sing won in the end. Our decision was based on the conclusion that being polite was more important than our embarrassment. The problem is, Song is being forced to write the first draft.

It's unfair. But that's fine.

Omniscient Reader's Viewpoint was written with that mindset.

One erases a sentence that the other person has thought about for a long time. One fills in a blank space the other person has left empty on purpose.

Every time we wondered what it means for two people to write one story, we considered the versions of *Omniscient Reader's Viewpoint* that might be being written in different parallel universes. Dokja, Junghyeok, Suyeong, Sangah...and all the other characters could talk and act differently in each version of *Omniscient Reader's Viewpoint.*

The part being erased in our story might be written into a story in a different universe, and the part being erased in a different universe might be written into our story. It's better to think some stories are written this way.

I sometimes take the time to reread the script I had to write in a rush. And I finally understand the other author who has written this story with me. I realize that a brick they took away didn't destroy the pillar I erected.

And at that moment, *Omniscient Reader's Viewpoint* becomes a totally different story from what I'd thought it was.

There are things we can only see when we encroach on each other, much in the way a puzzle is completed when the concave and convex pieces are put together. Surprisingly, the process enables us to say this.

"If it's you, I'm okay with it, even though it's a bit unfair to me."

It seems that rewriting and rereading aren't so different. The difference between author and reader is not so significant, just as a new story is born whenever readers read *Omniscient Reader's Viewpoint.* The coolest thing people can do together is create a story.

singNsong's *Omniscient Reader's Viewpoint* and the readers' *Omniscient Reader's Viewpoint* may not be the same story. We vaguely guess at the shape of another person's story pieces with our own story pieces in mind. It's all good.

It would be great if this story which we and you share can be a comfort to you on a lonely day.

We really appreciate all the people who choose to get involved with this story, out of the many other stories out there.

From singNsong, November 2021

Follow Dokja's story in full color, brought to life by the studio behind *Solo Leveling* !

Omniscient Reader's Viewpoint (Comic)

For more action-packed titles from REDICE STUDIO...

Solo Leveling (Comic)

The World After the Fall (Comic)

Tomb Raider King (Comic)

Overgeared (Comic)

Visit izepress.com for more information!